Also by Audrey Kalman

What Remains Unsaid
Dance of Souls

TINY SHOES DANCING

....

AND OTHER STORIES

AUDREY KALMAN

Terrella Media, Inc.
SAN MATEO, CALIFORNIA

Terrella Media, Inc.
816 Nevada Avenue
San Mateo, CA 94402

Publisher's Note: This is a work of fiction. Names, characters, places, and incidents are a product of the author's imagination. Locales and public names are sometimes used for atmospheric purposes. Any resemblance to actual people, living or dead, or to businesses, companies, events, institutions, or locales is completely coincidental.

Book layout © 2017 BookDesignTemplates.com
Cover design: Wendy Walter

Ordering Information:
Quantity sales. Special discounts are available on quantity purchases by corporations, associations, and others. For details, contact the Special Sales Department at the address above.

Tiny Shoes Dancing and Other Stories/Audrey Kalman.
1st edition
ISBN 978-1-7320546-9-1

For storytellers everywhere

CONTENTS

"Back After a Break to Discuss the Decline of Civilization" first appeared in *Boundoff*, Issue 105, October 15, 2014

"Bad Luck with Cats" first appeared in *Every Day Fiction*, April 13, 2013

"Before There Was a Benjamin" first appeared in *Sixfold*, Fiction Issue, Winter 2015

"Forget Me, Forget Me Not" first appeared in *Punchnel's*, July 3, 2013

"If Only You Weren't So" first appeared in *Mash Stories*, 2015

"Mistress Mine" first appeared in *Fault Zone: Stepping Up to the Edge*, Sand Hill Review Press, 2012

"Pearls" first appeared in *Fault Zone: Transform*, Sand Hill Review Press, 2017

"Pudding" first appeared in *Mash Stories*, 2016

"Put the Sweater on the Dog" first appeared in *Sand Hill Review*, 2015

"Skyping with the Rabbi" first appeared in *The Jewish Literary Journal*, 2014

"So She Says" first appeared in *Mash Stories*, 2015

"The Appointed Time and Place" first appeared in *Mash Stories*, 2016

"The Boy in the Window" first appeared in *Carry the Light: An Anthology*

"The Bureau of Lost Earrings" first appeared in *Pithead Chapel*, Volume 6, No. 1, January, 2017

"Tiny Shoes Dancing" first appeared in *Sand Hill Review*

"When All Else Fails" is excerpted from *What Remains Unsaid*, Sand Hill Review Press, 2017

TINY SHOES DANCING

....

AND OTHER STORIES

TINY SHOES DANCING

J ODY is not prone to praying, but she is praying now.

As the parent of a performer, she has been accorded practically a front-row seat. The location doesn't feel like such a favor anymore. The male lead has just knocked on the cottage door and moved aside in a *glissade dessous*. From where Jody sits she sees the rise and fall of his chest, the quiver at the tips of his outstretched fingers, his double blink as he anticipates Jody's daughter Adeline throwing open the door and stepping through as Giselle.

Adeline is seconds from missing her cue.

The orchestra plays the next bar. As the single note swells toward resolution, only the corps, the director, and Jody know that the door already ought to have been flung back. Beside her, Nick relaxes in the attitude of a proud and oblivious father. The dance critic in the balcony suspects nothing yet, though she would just as soon pen a story of scandal as one of triumph.

Jody calculates the moments by counting her heartbeats. There is still time, if Adeline appears now, for no one to notice a thing. A few more seconds and it will be too late.

§

Jody gave her daughter a name that would allow her to skim the stage like an angel. Not a name like her own, which sounds like work boots thumping on a dirty floor.

All the flexibility and possibility Jody had lost by the time she became a mother revealed itself in Adeline. Still, Jody hadn't pushed her daughter to begin ballet. Maybe she had admired a picture of Suzanne Farrell and yes, she'd taken Adeline to see *The Nutcracker* when she was three. But the desire sprang from Adeline herself, who nagged her mother for months before her fourth birthday.

"I want to do dancing. Please can I do dancing?" she asked, tilting into a pirouette that continued until she listed to the floor.

They began going once a week to Mrs. C-G's Dance Studio. Mrs. C-G was actually Mrs. Cartwright-Graczinski, an Iowa girl who had moved to New York in the 'seventies. There she had excelled at classical ballet to just the level at which she attracted the attention of Polish prodigy Kacper Graczinski. She joined her corn-fed beauty to his Slavic stoicism with a hyphen, settled in the suburbs, and opened her school.

Before Adeline started kindergarten, Jody took her to the morning ballet class for preschoolers. Jody sat on a wooden bench with the other mothers, peering into the studio through an interior wall of glass. Adeline's little feet pointed and flexed and Jody felt the flexion and extension of some long-dormant

12

muscle in herself. Jody thought Adeline had a natural grace lacking in the other little girls.

"Not every child can go on to a career in dance," Mrs. C-G told the mothers on the first day. "But ballet training is a strong foundation for *any* future athletic activity. And for life!" she added. Her zest would have seemed insincere coming from anyone else.

Jody, of course, had seen the ballet based on the fairy tale of a vainglorious orphan girl enslaved by her red shoes. The shoes, possessed of their own will, grew fast to the orphan girl's feet. They took her dancing ceaselessly in directions she did not want to go. Peace came only when she begged an executioner to chop off her feet and the red shoes with them.

But Adeline's shoes were cream satin and brushed the floor with the sound of an expelled sigh.

"I never want to be that mother," Jody said to her friend Ellen, who lived down the street and had two boys. The boys spent their days falling from the tops of bunk beds and transferring muck from the corners of the back yard to Ellen's kitchen floor.

"What mother?" Ellen asked.

"You know. The stage mother. The one who pushes. If *she* wants to do it, I'll support her, but I never want her to feel like it's something *I* want."

But where did the line leave off between the support and the push? When Adeline was seven, she said she wanted to move up to the next level. Mrs. C-G pointed out that meant attending practice five days a week instead of two. Jody remembered Adeline's solemn head with her dark chignon nodding.

After several months, Adeline began complaining. "Do I have to go to dance today? I want to go to Emmie's house after school."

"You know Mrs. C-G needs you to practice," Jody said. "How are you going to be a famous ballerina if you don't practice?"

"I don't want to be a famous ballerina!"

Still, Adeline continued pirouetting through the house.

At nine, she outgrew Mrs. C-G. With great sadness, the teacher wrote out the name and number of a Manhattan school. And so began their daily afternoon subway rides to The New York Academy of Classical Dance.

At twelve, Adeline added Saturdays to her practice schedule as all the Level 6 students were required to do. Jody and Nick took Adeline to the Academy at nine in the morning and spent the day together in Manhattan. "Bonus time," Nick called it, and mapped out routes to restaurants and museums as though they were on a holiday.

"Sophie takes the train by herself," Adeline said one day not long after her thirteenth birthday.

"Sophie's almost fifteen!" Jody said.

Adeline pouted and turned her face away.

Jody sighed. "When you're fourteen, we'll talk about it."

§

A thousand times, Jody has watched Adeline's rehearsals and performances. She has seen her daughter's shoes sweep across the stage and felt the thrilling rise as her foot arches into that anatomical impossibility, *en pointe*.

Jody has saved every pair of dance shoes Adeline ever wore. She keeps them in a closet under the stairs, the kind of closet where a naughty girl in a fairy tale might be forced to live.

Sometimes, Jody goes to sit in the closet among the boxes. She always does it when no one else is home. The boxes, lined on the shelves in chronological order, look practically new, unlike the shoes they contain. She doesn't even need to open a box to picture the shoes within and recall how Adeline looked wearing them.

At first, Adeline went through only a couple pairs a year. Since beginning daily practices, she needs new ones every month. Once, when Adeline was thirteen and had just worn through her first pair of size sevens, Jody sat in the closet and tried to put her foot into one. Although seven was ostensibly her own shoe size, Jody's foot spread nearly twice the width of her daughter's shoe. Still, she forced both shoes onto her feet and tried to rise up *en pointe*.

The first time Adeline took the train alone, Jody sat at the kitchen table doing nothing for forty-seven minutes, precisely the amount of time she calculated it would take the 2:56 to arrive at Grand Central and Adeline to walk the three blocks to the Academy. At minute fifty-two, Jody dialed Adeline's cell phone number.

Her daughter answered after three rings.

"Oh—hi, Mom," she said in a tone that managed to sound both snarky and guilty. "Sorry I forgot to call."

§

Tonight, there is no number Jody can call to check on Adeline. She must be behind the cottage door. Where else would she be? Jody did not see her at the theatre before the show. But that was not unusual. Adeline is sixteen and a half now and a pro on the train. She left their house early in the afternoon without showing her face to say goodbye. Jody heard the front door slam.

"Bye, honey!" Jody called through the closed door. She no longer expected a response, but could not seem to stifle her impulse to say goodbye.

Joshua Sanderson. That's the name of the male lead. He is a beautiful boy. He has been dancing since he was five. That he managed not to break some bone during the long arc of boyhood impresses Jody no end. She hardly knows Mrs. Sanderson, despite years of seeing her at the Academy and at performances. Jody thinks Adeline might have "a thing" for Joshua.

The audience, though not yet conscious of looming disaster, is beginning to stir.

§

Recently, Jody seems to have something real to worry about. Adeline's body, which had been late to puberty, finally softened as much as a body whose muscles are worked for nine hours a day can soften. Almost as soon as this happened Adeline began eating less—an orange for breakfast, yogurt for lunch, a diet shake before rehearsal. When she comes home late from the Academy, she takes the plate Jody has warmed for her straight to her room. Emptying the bathroom wastebasket one day, Jody noticed a putrid smell and found a slimy chicken breast coated in sauce at the bottom of the bag.

She probably should sit Adeline down and have a talk. "Honey," she should say, "I'm worried about you." But when she tries to picture it, the words fly over her daughter's head and Adeline gives her that sideways look. The words are a poor substitute for the ones fluttering inside Jody's head: *anorexia, bulimia*. Such ugly conditions described by such beautiful syllables, as beautiful as her tall, dark-haired daughter with her chiseled cheeks and prominent collarbones.

Jody stares with the rest of the audience into the empty space on stage where Adeline should be. Suddenly, she feels the weight of her daughter as a toddler in her arms. When Adeline fell asleep on car rides, Jody sacrificed her own weak back to wrest her daughter from the booster seat and lug her inside the house to bed.

Jody's concern over Adeline acquired a sudden and pressing actuality two nights before the opening performance of Giselle.

Nick laid his book face down on the bedspread and looked at her over his reading glasses. "What's going on with Adeline? She's skin and bones."

It sounded to Jody like an accusation. "Some crazy diet, I guess. You know how they pressure the girls about their weight."

"We should talk to her."

Jody drew her knees up under the sheet. Nick's book slid sideways and collapsed on itself, losing his place.

"Not before the opening," she said. "We can't upset her."

"Let's take her somewhere afterwards, then. Katz's."

Jody didn't know whether to laugh or cry at the idea of taking an anorexic to a deli, but she nodded.

Only now, after everyone else in the audience has sensed that something is wrong, does Nick grasp Jody's forearm with an urgency she hasn't felt from him in years.

§

A full ten seconds have passed. The cottage door, actually a block of grayish-brown foam, remains closed. Joshua, dipping his knees and raising his arms, makes a slight movement with his head as if he wants to look over his shoulder.

Then Jody sees, or thinks she sees, a fluttering of the backstage curtain. A moment later, a girl's body emerges. Jody gasps when she realizes it's not Adeline.

Watching the understudy glide across the stage in Adeline's place, Jody is sure that the shoes at home have escaped their boxes and the closet as well. If she returns now she will find hundreds of dance shoes in all sizes skimming the carpet, tripping up the stairs, brushing the marble floor of the bathroom, and sinking themselves into the fluffy rug on the floor of Adeline's room.

Adeline's room.

Jody stands so quickly that heads turn. She shrugs off the clutch of Nick's fingers and bangs her head on the seat in front of her as she bends to grab her purse from the floor.

The shoes are everywhere now. They have left the house and arrived at the theater. Most are pink or cream-colored but one pair, from Adeline's thirteenth year, is a deep rose, the color of blood dried on white fabric. The deep rose shoes dance in the aisle, taunting and summoning. Jody shimmies over knees and feet to exit the row.

The rose shoes *plié* again and again, waiting for Jody. As soon as she reaches them, they dart toward the exit door at the back of the theater. She is running now. Her feet thump on the floor and people turn to look at her. The other shoes swarm around her—*couru, fouetté, pas de bourrée*—urging her on.

Nick stumbles after her. "Jody!" he shrieks.

She is the performance now: the insane stage mother disrupting the precise bowing of the violins and the actions of the hero busy saving the day on stage.

The exit door swings open with a wail that doesn't stop. Jody is wailing now too, following shoes, pursued by shoes, on her way to her daughter's room and the round white rug onto which Adeline will have slumped with the blood blossoming from her ankles.

■ ■ ■

. . . .

FORGET ME, FORGET ME NOT

She measures her pace by the whisper of her footfalls in the dust. Four steps for every inbreath, four steps for every outbreath.

She swallows the next-to-last energy gel at mile 33. Seven easy ones to go with few gentle hills, nothing like the monster between miles 18 and 22.

What remains of her mind hovers five feet off the ground. It expands with the inbreath, empties with the outbreath. Which is why she began running in the first place: to arrive at the forgetting.

A body can only take so much, her mama said.

Take that, body, Lilah whispers.

The dry seedpods of the grasses prickle her calves. She has been running since sunrise. Here, the trail leads out of the woods to a field where deer sleep at night, leaving ovals of flattened grass. No deer now, only the midday screech of cicadas.

She has travelled this trail before with fellow runners. Much as she hates going over ground already covered, the repetition makes running alone now feel safer. She knows the open space will close again in another mile. She will finish in deep woods long before the sun goes down and Paul will pick her up at the appointed roadside spot. He'll already have turned the car to face homeward. On the drive back, he won't shut up about how impressed he is that she can do this.

She sucks down the last gel at mile 36, already deep in the woods. Shade blankets her shoulders.

Maybe it's the shadows flickering across her eyes with each step or her empty hovering mind not paying attention. In any event the small gray rock can hardly be blamed for taking the impact of her foot.

Lilah stumbles and shrieks when her leg gives. The spectacular separation of ligaments seems to occur at quarter-speed. She has known such moments before, when events unfold with the luxurious slowness of a car wreck. The things a body can take when all is forgotten.

She piles injury on injury, landing on her thigh with enough impact to bruise. The cicadas have fallen silent. She listens to her breath. She is no stranger to pain but finds she must continue making noise, a kind of moaning, to cope with the sensation in her ankle. Her mind is a genie back in its bottle, an imprisoned dynamo churning out thoughts. Next week's race, which now cannot be run; her fellow runners, who will smother her with sympathy. And the disappointment of Paul.

Paul, right now, is driving to the meeting place. He has never once forgotten, or betrayed irritation at what surely must be an inconvenience, just as he has never grown impatient during the months he has been waiting to touch her. All her wounds, inside and now outside, he has patiently observed without probing.

A body can only take so much, she whispered to him.

Lilah folds her good leg under her and uses the power of her well-trained quadriceps to push herself to standing. Her gimp leg throbs and dangles. When she sets its toe on the path and tries to take a step, her body screams for her.

Only minutes have passed since she was lolloping through the forest with the abandon of a deer. Yet the shadows seem to have lengthened. Will Paul come for her, through the shadows, if she calls? The final yes or no seems random, to be arrived at by plucking petals from the daisy's center.

She sinks onto the leafy dust of the path.

The gray rock of her undoing sits silent, so like a stone. She understands now that a body can take anything at all, but the mind—the mind is another story altogether.

■ ■ ■

BACK AFTER A BREAK TO
DISCUSS THE DECLINE OF
CIVILIZATION

P RESTON interrupted Marilee just as she began to describe her dream.

"Does the trash company take batteries?" he asked.

The dream seemed irrelevant by the time she finished answering. In it, Preston had kissed another woman. That was it—just kissed—but she had spent the remainder of the night bereft.

They would be married twenty-six years on Sunday. Next week the trash company was coming for a big-item pick-up, which entitled them to rid themselves of one large appliance, one piece of furniture, and twelve bags or bundles. They had spent the morning excavating the garage.

Preston disappeared into the house. Marilee waited for him on the threshold of the open garage. Two minutes passed, then five. Her neighbor, Jilly, walked by with her Doberman. Marilee opened her mouth to call hello before she noticed Jilly was on her cell phone, looking straight ahead and nodding to the voice coming through the Bluetooth. Marilee closed her mouth and watched the dog's high, tight ass prance away up the sidewalk.

After a while Marilee walked around to the back yard. This was her territory. In the early years of their marriage she had wielded a shovel to soften the clay soil with compost and shears to tame the hedge separating their house from Jilly's. Now they paid gardeners for that. Preston came back here only when they threw a party. He'd stand at the outdoor kitchen grill and flip the steaks she had selected, purchased, and seasoned.

Marilee extracted her iPod from her pocket, untangled the cord, and pressed the buds into her ears. The gardeners trimmed and raked but always neglected the weeding. She had work to do.

§

She had no idea whether her marriage was solid as bedrock or drifting like an ice floe into open ocean. How did people decide? For years, she knew no one who had gotten divorced. Now every other e-mail from a friend seemed to begin, "I have some unhappy news…" But the women popped up refreshed from the ashes of their marriages, sporting new clothes and stylish haircuts. Dating, even.

Once, Marilee had watched Preston kiss other women, and not in a dream. It happened before they got engaged. He had appetites and she wanted to prove she was a liberated woman. She went with him to a strip club.

She found herself not knowing where to look. At the dancer flirting with the pole? At the gentlemen panting after the dancer? She looked at Preston. He was looking at another woman. No, not just looking. Beckoning. The woman came to their table and leaned close to hear Preston over the music. Marilee's eyes jumped from pole dancer to men to her boyfriend's shag of hair and landed on the woman's cleavage. The crevasse sucked her into its shadow.

There were other strip clubs, other lap dances, until they got engaged and agreed, without speaking of it, to act respectably. The swinging 'Seventies were over. It was time to settle down, ride out the recession, turn their attention to Wall Street.

But once more in the early years of marriage, before the girls were born, she had watched him kiss another woman.

§

Preston would be upstairs on the computer. He hadn't yet retired, as she had, so he still had work important enough to invade his Saturday morning. Marilee pictured him slumped before the screen, chin outthrust, index finger tapping the mouse, then leaning back, yawning, scratching the strip of belly exposed when his shirt rode up.

If Preston had looked out the window he would have seen Marilee crouching at the base of the hedge like a burglar or a tribal shaman. She began yanking out shoots of Bermuda grass. She knew she shouldn't—the very tiniest of broken stems could re-propagate—but retrieving the weeding rake and trowel from the garage seemed too troublesome.

She readjusted her iPod's left ear bud.

"Looking back even further into the past," the interviewer was saying to the psychologist on the radio show, "you claim we're now living in the most peaceful period in human history."

The psychologist chronicled the statistics leading to this conclusion. Marilee rested her knees on the grass and wiped her palms on her thighs. If peace was breaking out around the world, what accounted for everyone's sense that society was running down to its dregs? The human brain must be splendidly designed for the purpose of manufacturing misery.

She tugged at the clump of Bermuda grass. It first resisted and then separated at the soil line, leaving its rhizomes intact underground to fight another day.

§

In the dream, the woman had turned away from Marilee with a look that said, I'll kiss your husband but I won't kiss you.

There had been a time when she and Preston both had fallen a little in love with a lab assistant at Preston's work. This was in the early years of their marriage when love and lust were mixed up together and the residue of experimentation still clung to them.

Her name was Cassandra, but everyone called her Cassie.

"She's kind of a party animal," Preston said.

"Does she have a boyfriend?" Marilee asked.

"That guy she brought to the Christmas party was the last one I knew about. She dumped him."

"You wouldn't think she'd have trouble finding another one."

Marilee and Preston talked about Cassie this way for months. They were the worldly couple looking out for young

Cassie's future. Then Cassie invited them for a weekend at her parents' place in Santa Barbara. They arrived expecting another couple, or at least the illusory boyfriend, but Cassie was alone.

Cassie had kissed them both.

§

Marilee was hearing every other sentence or so of the interview, as if her mind was an imperfectly tuned radio receiver. "It's a question of empathy. Are you *always* on the side of the angels? Is your enemy *always* evil?" one of the interviewees was saying.

Preston and Marilee had sent their younger daughter off to college three months ago. Some of Marilee's friends spoke about the liberation that accompanied their children's leave-taking. Others described the desolation of the empty nest. Marilee already had cleared out Tina's room and moved in a crafting table. The drawback to this arrangement was the room's proximity to Preston's office, which had once belonged to their older daughter. An angel beside evil—but which was which?

The interviewer's voice gave way to music. She listened so often to this particular show that the interlude felt like part of her being. She liked the musical theme and wouldn't have minded if it had lengthened into a song. But fifteen seconds was all you got.

The other interviewee spoke. "I'm not saying there's not awful violence going on. It's dreadful. But is it more dreadful than it used to be?"

Marilee hugged the pile of pulled Bermuda grass close on her way to the compost bin. When she reached the bin she

27

realized she had gone about things backwards. She would have to put down the grass to open the bin.

The interviewer said, "Look closely at the numbers. They don't lie—the past is a lot less innocent than it seems."

She stared at the green plastic lid as if she could lift it by force of will, then closed her eyes.

§

Cassie's face had felt very small between Marilee's hands. She wondered whether this was how her own face felt when Preston laid his palms against her cheeks and guided her in for a kiss.

"You think too much," Cassie said. "The both of you."

It surprised Marilee how foggy Santa Barbara was in the morning. Outside Cassie's parents' house, where the beach should have been, there was only a shimmering curtain of vapor.

§

When Marilee opened her eyes, the lid *was* up, not by force of will but by Preston.

Marilee dumped the Bermuda grass into the bin and plucked the ear buds from her ears. The sounds of the world rushed back: an airplane, a blue jay, traffic, Jilly's dog barking on the other side of the fence, her husband's voice.

Preston waved a piece of paper before her.

"Honey, I found the information on hazardous waste," he said.

He knelt and began to gather stray strands of grass that had drifted to the ground outside the bin. Marilee sank down beside him and together they used the hazardous waste printout as a scoop.

Preston stood. His head momentarily blocked the sun, making a flat black outline of his face and shoulders. Marilee reached for his extended hand.

"Don't worry," he said. "I'll take care of everything."

The Bermuda grass, she saw, had stained her palms the color of envy.

▩ ▩ ▩

BEFORE THERE WAS A BENJAMIN

MAAAAAAMAAAAAA!"
Benjamin's voice streams into Melinda's ear, a pure vibration of pain palpable even from downstairs. She meant only to check on the roasting chicken, only for a moment, but the peace of the kitchen captivated her and she lingered.

"Mama's coming, Ben," she calls from halfway up the stairs. She knows that the scream, as piercing and pained as it is, signifies nothing more dire than frustration. And yes, here he is, just where she left him on the floor of his room, surrounded by Lego bricks. The spire they have been working on has toppled from its base onto the carpet. Benjamin sits helpless before the disaster. He must have pressed too hard trying to add onto the top. Tears smudge his cheeks.

"Maaaamaaa," he says again, more softly.

"Mama's here, honey," Melinda says, and tries not to sigh audibly or let visions of other ten-year-old boys playing with their friends cloud her mind. "We'll make it again. I'll steady it and you can put more bricks on top."

The Lego Disaster leads with wearisome inevitably to the Chicken Disaster. Melinda becomes more absorbed than she imagined would be possible in constructing the delicate blue-red-blue-red-blue tower. Benjamin insists on the precise alternation of colors. Her job becomes picking out and setting aside the single blue and red bricks. Benjamin's fingers work clumsily—singles being the most difficult to manipulate and the most tenuously connected—and the tower collapses twice more before rising successfully.

Only when she opens the door of Benjamin's room and smells burnt rosemary and the choking char of chicken skin does she remember.

"Shit! Shit, shit, shit!" Melinda covers her mouth, but it's too late.

"Shit what, Mama?" Benjamin asks.

"The chicken. Dinner. Burnt to a crisp."

"Can I see?"

"Oh, sure. Let's everybody ogle Mama's mistake."

Benjamin trails her down the stairs into the kitchen, which is anything but a sanctuary now. Smoke creeps from around the oven door. Benjamin's presence lends foreboding to the room's ordinary objects: the knives in their wooden block, the corkscrew beside the wine rack. Melinda would give anything for a glass of wine, but it's barely past three and there's no drinking until six-thirty when Peter gets off work. That's the deal they made. Peter makes the money and carries the health insurance. Melinda cares for Benjamin when he gets home from his program, makes the dinner, and forgoes mid-afternoon glasses of wine. She needs to remain vigilant as long as she's the only adult in the house. Only now she has to figure out something else for dinner because she can see, when she opens the oven door, that the chicken is as ruined as she feared.

§

Long before there was a Benjamin, Melinda saw a man playing guitar. The man's black hair rippled down his back. A silver and turquoise bracelet flashed on his wrist when he strummed.

Had Melinda believed in either divinity or retribution, she would have thought Benjamin must be divine retribution for—what, exactly? Perhaps for the abandon with which she gave herself to Peter that first night, combing his long hair with trembling fingers, or for their years-long courtship, or the years-long, fitful process of conceiving their only son.

§

Nobody ever thinks theirs will be the star-child. That's what Tara calls Benjamin. Tara met Benjamin when he was just a baby. He looked up at her from his blue flannel swaddle and gave her the first smile he ever gave anyone. Later, three years old and still pre-verbal, he managed somehow to communicate that he wanted Tara to push him in the stroller. When words finally came, he asked for her, *Auntie Tata*, and Auntie Tata she remained.

Tara was from Peter's life before, a singer with short spiky hair and a winsome overbite. Peter swore up and down, even all these years later, that he'd never slept with her. Melinda tolerated Tara for a long time because she was part of Peter's life. Then she started to like Tara. Gradually, the triangle realigned. Now the two women are friends, often bemoaning Peter's obtuse male energy. These days, Melinda sees Tara during the day while Peter is at work and doesn't mention Tara to him when he comes home.

She calls Tara to report the Chicken Disaster.

"Oh, sweetie," Tara says. "I'm so sorry. I'll bring you a deli chicken on my way to rehearsal tonight. Peter won't know the difference."

Benjamin grabs Tara's hand the moment she walks in and leads her upstairs to show off the Lego creation. Melinda stays downstairs and pours the wine, which is okay now that there's another adult in the house.

"Ben, do you want to watch your show?" Melinda asks when he comes downstairs with Tara. He jumps and pinwheels his arms, screeching, "My show! My show!"

In the kitchen with her glass of wine, her friend, and the purchased chicken in the scrubbed-out oven, *on low*, Melinda feels for a moment like the mother she once imagined she would be.

"You think I shouldn't let him watch," she says.

Tara stretches her arms overhead with a cat-like languor available only to single, childfree women. "Hey, sweetie, you do what you gotta do. But he's special, that one."

They have some variation of this conversation every time they meet. Tara has always seen beneath the skin of the world. Her eyes, when she looks at Benjamin, seem sharp and coppery, like the colored spikes of her hair.

"You should bring him to a *real* show," Tara says. "I've got some local ones coming up."

"Are you kidding? He couldn't sit still."

"He wouldn't have to. He can dance with everybody else."

Melinda lets the idea rest without responding, but the picture of her excitable son at a Daughters of the Milky Way concert, tossing his hefty body into the swaying crowd, stays with her.

§

Before there was a Benjamin, according to Tara, there was a swirling colorful energy that danced through the universe, connected with all other energies, loved and loving, empathic, in-place, at home. Benjamin's troubles began only after he was embodied, only after sperm met egg and created the specific physical manifestation that became *Benjamin* and slipped—nay, struggled—into this world on a frigid December morning a full month before he had been scheduled to arrive.

Melinda recalls those first weeks of Benjamin's life: how startled she was every time she found his Isolette in the NICU and him encased within, sensors monitoring his breath and a tube delivering him food as if he'd been hatched, not birthed. How she sat in a rocking chair beside the Isolette, hooked like a cow to the rhythmically whining breast pump, extracting milk that was fed to him first through the tube and then with an eye dropper and finally from a bottle. How, when the doctors declared him well enough to go home and Peter pushed her in a wheelchair with Benjamin in her arms down to the hospital's entrance she felt an overwhelming desire to stay in the place that had kept her child alive for two weeks, as cold and isolating as it had been, because surely at home her ineptitude would kill him.

§

Melinda anticipates that Peter will think taking Benjamin to a concert is a terrible idea. She brings it up on a Sunday morning, which didn't used to be a good time to discuss anything since he would be hung over and spaced out till late afternoon. Now, as the manager of the electronics department at Great Gadgets, he has to maintain a schedule. He gets up before Melinda on weekends and takes the first shift with Benjamin, letting his son help make pancakes.

Melinda comes into a kitchen dusted with flour. She presses her palms into her eyes.

"There's coffee," Peter says, partially redeeming himself.

When Benjamin was four and had just said "Dada" for the first time, Peter played his last gig and gave himself a haircut. Melinda remembers watching her husband through the open bathroom door as he gathered up the sheaf of hair and went after it with scissors. He might have needed comforting but even then, only four years into motherhood, she was fresh out of extra cheer. Peter dropped the sheared hair into the bathroom wastebasket and ran his hand through what remained on his head. He'd had to go in for a professional trim before he interviewed at Great Gadgets.

Melinda sips her coffee and wonders what happened to the Melinda who followed Peter from gig to gig, sleeping in two-star motels or sometimes on the bus. It's obvious if she thinks about it: motherhood happened. And not just garden-variety motherhood but one defined by the revelation of who Benjamin was and what he would demand of her. She acquired expertise she didn't want, insisting on appointments with specialists, arguing with the insurance company, negotiating the public school bureaucracy. She spent hours in plastic chairs outside the principal's office like a naughty child. She maintained a dossier of experts and resources. She experienced the swell of hope accompanying each step forward, the subsequent evaporation of hope, the acceptance that there was no hope.

And the bills, always the bills. The arguments with Peter about whether she should go back to work to help with the cost of Benjamin's program. Running every little bit of her son's life, her husband's life, her own life, scripting, managing, managing, until she wasn't managing at all.

Melinda tries to picture Peter's long hair as she watches him frying pancakes. Probably better it's short; who would want hairs falling in the batter? But imagining her husband as he once was is the only way she can bring herself to talk about the concert. Maybe, if she presents the idea in just the right way, he'll think it's brilliant. Maybe he'll even come with them.

"So, Benjamin has been getting more into music lately," she says. She waits a moment before adding, "We've been listening to some of your songs."

Peter drags the spatula across the pan, no doubt scratching bits of Teflon into their food. "Oh really?"

"And he's been wanting to fool around on the keyboard."

The electric keyboard has sat for years in the corner of the living room. Peter bought it when Benjamin was a year old. He would hold his son on his lap and guide Benjamin's fingers from note to note. As soon as Benjamin could move, he slithered off his father's lap and crawled away.

"Haven't you, honey?" Melinda asks her son, who is forking pancake into his mouth. Then, to Peter, "Tara's playing in a few weeks. I was thinking he might enjoy that."

Peter jiggles the pan. "A concert," he says, as if she had suggested taking their son to a leper colony.

Melinda turns to Benjamin. "Would you like to go to a concert, Ben? And hear *live music*?"

She knows this tactic is unfair, eliciting her son's enthusiasm to override her husband's reservations, but she feels suddenly trapped and spiteful. Who is Peter to tell them what to do when his interactions with Benjamin are limited to Sunday morning pancakes followed by a cartoon marathon?

Tara's idea that became Benjamin's desire has become Melinda's need. She must take Benjamin to this concert.

"Yefff, confert!" Benjamin says enthusiastically through a mouthful of pancake. Peter says nothing, and the possibility that they might all go together evaporates.

§

Before there was a Benjamin there was a flawed world hurtling toward ruin. Who would want to bring a child into such a world? Peter asked, first in his songs and then directly of Melinda. She had no good answer but the ringing imperative of her biology. Feeling more than thinking, feeling she must, *or else*, Melinda sweet-talked Peter into ditching the birth control, as women have always done who are driven by needs more urgent than their need for love.

Years later, seeking an explanation for Benjamin, she read about Indigos and Crystals and Rainbows on Web sites with names like mystarchild.com and starchildren.net. *Star Children are the hope of humanity.* Melinda went hot, then cold, then hot again with the revelation that forces other than biology might be at work. Knowing what he had the potential to become, how could she *not* have brought Benjamin into this world?

She kept her knowledge hidden from Peter. For all the mind-expanding drugs and body-shattering rock 'n' roll of his youth, Peter had turned into a person who believed only what he could see or touch or hear, only what could be measured. "Charlatans," he snarled when she made an appointment for Benjamin with a holistic nutritionist. If she mentioned an herbal supplement that might improve their son's ability to sit still, Peter said, "Show me the studies." Melinda added *advocate* to the list of roles she had not asked for.

Neither had she asked to be the person standing between two worlds, and yet here she was, an umbilical cord to the universe. She sometimes played a version of the *Would you rather...?* game with herself. Only instead of the absurd dichotomies posed by her teenage friends—would you rather get eaten alive by a lion or pushed out of a plane without a parachute?— she wondered: would she rather have given birth to a son afflicted with cancer? cystic fibrosis? blood that wouldn't clot? Melinda even began contemplating the value of a higher power who would have borne responsibility for Benjamin's condition and could have promised a state of perfect grace.

Melinda uses her imagination, too, to project Benjamin into a future without her, as if anxiety could forestall disaster. Will he ever get a job? Find an apartment? Make friends? Fall in love? She now lives in a future she failed to imagine during that first blessed year with roly-poly Benjamin, when nobody worried that he did not speak because he was not yet expected to and the hope had still been there that he would grow into the boy of her imagining.

Before there was a Benjamin there was the potential energy of a Benjamin: drawn, lifted, poised with promise at the edge of this world.

§

Melinda decides on a Friday night concert, for no reason other than it means she won't have to see Peter before they leave. When the tickets arrive in the mail, Melinda slits the envelope with a long silver letter opener and slips them under a folder of coupons in the kitchen drawer. She looks forward to going and relishes sneaking around to do it. She tries to recall the last time she and Peter went to a concert but her mind fills with a jumble of images without dates or context.

The concert will end well past Benjamin's bedtime. She tries to get him to take a nap after she picks him up from his program but he won't lie down. She runs through her little bag of survival tricks. Building him a Hot Wheels track buys her a half hour while he races every car in his collection around it. Then he requires her help for an hour picking up the cars he has dumped onto the floor. Each one must be examined and categorized and aligned on the shelf in an exact but incomprehensible order. These obligations seem less burdensome with the promise of the concert ahead. Melinda hums a song from Tara's latest CD as she lowers an orange Chevy beside a blue Dodge.

At five-thirty, Melinda feeds Benjamin dinner. Her already-knotted stomach won't allow her to eat. Daughters of the Milky Way goes on at nine, after the warm-up band, and the club is an hour's drive from their house. It seems they ought to have plenty of time, but Benjamin dawdles over the chicken nuggets and Melinda begins to worry they will still be home when Peter arrives. She glances at her watch as Benjamin pushes the last of the crumb-crusted bits into a smear of ketchup and then hustles him to the car without even washing his hands.

Melinda plays Tara's CD as they drive. She glimpses Benjamin in the rearview mirror, swaying to the beat.

"We'll see Auntie Tata in a little while, honey," Melinda says. "We might not get to talk to her, though. She'll be up on stage and we'll be watching her."

Benjamin continues bobbing his head as if he's nodding. He needs a haircut—his bangs swish in front of his eyes—and Melinda sighs with the ceaseless effort of keeping her son anchored to this world. She has to cut his hair herself; he can't tolerate sitting in the barber chair or the feeling of the hair-catching apron cinched around his neck. She cuts in dribs and drabs, a snip here while he pushes his toy boats around the bath, a clip there while he drifts to sleep. And now it dawns on her just how stupid she may be to take him to the concert, this child whose tolerance for the unfamiliar can be calibrated in millimeters, who is driven to distraction by the everyday: the elastic of his socks, the label in the collar of his shirt. Melinda can hear Peter's *I told you so*.

But it's too late to turn back. She promised her son a concert, *live music*, and Tara expects them. Melinda clings to the presence of Auntie Tata. Benjamin will be okay because Tara will be there.

It's dark when they arrive and Melinda finds parking in the small lot behind the club. She begins to understand that the evening is unraveling when she cannot coax Benjamin from the car. She somehow failed to consider his unpredictable propensity to become an immovable object, incapable of being acted upon by any force. She unbuckles his seat belt and stands beside the open car door. The CD is off but Benjamin tilts his head from side to side as if still keeping the beat. Melinda sighs loudly.

"Benjamin. Honey."

She knows from experience that nothing she feels like doing will be effective: cajoling, reasoning, pleading, reprimanding, yelling, or tugging his arm. Reluctantly, she shuts the car door and leans against it. *I can be a star-child too*, she thinks, a being oblivious to the physical world and the constraints of time. If she acts as if she has all the time in the universe, then Benjamin will catch up with her, but it's a tricky game. If he senses her exasperation he will remain rooted to his seat.

The silvery streetlight is too faint to illuminate her watch but she guesses it must be close to nine. She looks up at the stars, which tell her nothing of the passage of time. *Good,* she thinks. *Just as well. Now we can turn around and go home—no harm done.* At that moment Benjamin opens the car door, pressing it outward against Melinda's body.

The battle is not won yet. She holds his hand and they cross the gravel parking lot, slowly, listening to every crunch underfoot. She hears something else as they approach the building: the thump and strum of the warm-up band playing what must be its final number. The journey across the gravel takes them the full length of the song. Then, just as she thinks they are home free, Benjamin stops abruptly at the edge of the parking lot.

Melinda realizes he is transfixed by an arrangement of rocks around the base of a lamp post. What does he see there? The invisible energy of stone, a sprite darting in the shadows? Again Melinda waits. The music ends. She hears a door open nearby and the grind of footsteps. A man materializes in the indigo

41

shadow of the building only a few yards from where Benjamin crouches.

§

She's afraid for only a moment. Then she begins staring at the man as intently as Benjamin stares at the rocks. He looks a little like Willie Nelson with a craggy face and a ponytail down his back. He might be an incarnation of Peter twenty years hence.

The man is smoking a joint, something Melinda hasn't done since her early days with Peter. The smell of marijuana transports her instantly the way smells do, back to one of a hundred dim clubs where she sits at the bar waiting for Peter's band to go on. If she looks away from Benjamin it is possible to remember a time before there was a Benjamin, when she was simply *Melinda*, an agent of her own destiny, a container big enough for whatever emotion might pour through her, and not buffeted by the universe speaking through this fucking star-child it sent to test her.

The man approaches and holds out the joint. Benjamin is looking so hard at the rocks that he doesn't notice the man or his offering. Melinda thinks, *Ick—it's got his saliva all over it* and *I have to drive home later* and *I've heard weed is stronger now than it used to be.* These thoughts dissolve as she reaches to accept the joint. She can't see the color of the man's eyes or his hair except that it seems to shine with streaks of silver in the streetlight and shimmers through her tears.

The smoke sears her lungs. She holds it in for a heartbeat, then lets it stream out the side of her mouth before handing the joint to the man and turning back to her son.

"Benjamin, honey," she says. "Auntie Tata's music is going to start soon."

She grabs Benjamin's hand and pulls. He's a lump, as inert and fixed as the rocks he's examining. The man takes a final toke and tosses the joint to the ground, crushes it under his boot. A cowboy boot. All that's missing is the ten-gallon hat, but he has no hat, just his long, beautiful, shining silver hair, which Melinda wants suddenly to touch.

The man's voice shocks her back to the dilemma at hand.

"May I?"

He gestures toward Benjamin.

Now she has been more than stupid; she has been irresponsible. She'll have to explain to Peter not only the bone-headedness of bringing Benjamin here but of smoking pot and standing by while some stranger abducted him.

But a kidnapper would not ask for permission, nor would he bend down beside Benjamin and stare with him at the rocks as if expecting them to move or speak. She watches the two of them concentrate on the rocks. Their forms make a constellation of shadows.

From inside the club Melinda hears the first twangs of Tara's electric guitar followed by the clash of the high-hat. The melody of the song they have just been hearing on the car's stereo now bleeds through the club wall as Daughters of the Milky Way begins the first set. Tara will be scanning the crowd for them.

Benjamin turns toward the man. She sees his face uplifted in profile. The man spreads his arms and Benjamin moves into his embrace. The man stands with Benjamin wrapped around him like a baby monkey.

Melinda looks up at the sky and sees the actual Milky Way. At that moment, she can almost believe her son came from out there, that he is the star-child she sometimes wishes he were. She can almost believe that before there was a Benjamin there was a Melinda distinct and differentiated, separate but not alone, secure in her own embodiment. She can almost believe in signs and signals, in the thrilling happenstance of a man who might have come to her in a dream but instead comes to her in a gravel parking lot while inside her friend sings about stardust and substantiation.

The man looks at Melinda and nods toward the door of the club.

Benjamin lifts his head from the man's chest.

"Mama, come," he commands, and she does.

■ ■ ■

....

EVERYONE IS GONE

O WNING a Dollar Bin franchise wasn't making Luke Ralo wealthy, but he gave off the smell of having come from nothing. Barbara Timoney found his wispy moustache and uneven teeth endearing. Besides which, he was a philosopher, and he was always good for a laugh. Just that morning while she was checking out, he had shown her a plastic cherub on a key chain.

"Look, water goes here," he said, unscrewing the cherub's head. "Then, squish! He goes pee-pee! Very good for a joke."

Barbara lowered her chin to look over the top of her glasses and saw the plastic penis, barely thicker than a strand of spaghetti, through which the cherub was able to dispense such lusty entertainment among friends.

"Hmmph," she said. "I guess I'm too old to appreciate those kinds of jokes."

"No no no!" Luke fired off the words as enthusiastically as the cherub would likely spray the unsuspecting. "Always, you stay young in here." He thumped his fist on his chest. Then he shook out a plastic bag to stow her masking tape and steel wool soap pads. She handed him two dollars and sixteen cents and they smiled at each other.

§

At home, she found the cat up to his usual tricks. He was a rescue kitten who had come to Barbara small enough to rest in her palm and so young it was impossible to discern any outline of his future personality. For a week, he had mewed and shivered as she transitioned him from eyedroppers of milk to softened kibble. Then, seemingly overnight, Barbara found herself living with a 16-pound gray-and-white tuxedo who never met a soft paper product he didn't love.

Barbara saw the devastation the moment she opened the door. "Mr. Meow!" She used the voice she once had employed to get her students to sit down and pay attention. She followed the trail of shredded toilet tissue into her bedroom. Mr. Meow looked up from the bed, his white paws curved around the remains of the roll, and shook his head to dislodge a strand of tissue hanging from a whisker.

"Mr. Meow!" Barbara said again. This time she used the voice that preceded a call to the principal's office.

§

Barbara's daughter was coming for dinner. These visits were not Barbara's idea. She hadn't liked to cook when Annette was growing up but had put on a show of it, tearing Crock-Pot recipes from the newspaper and studying her copy of Betty

Crocker. When Annette left for college, Barbara felt lighter. She was unable to tell whether it was the relief of having delivered her daughter, close to 100-percent functional, to the world at large, or the fact that she would never again have to pretend to enjoy cooking.

Annette was a good girl. She knew enough to bring takeout from China Garden. Still, her visit necessitated vacuuming up the shreds of tissue. Where had Mr. Meow found that roll? Barbara thought every last one had been shut away. Luckily, the Dollar Bin sold toilet tissue for cheap.

Mr. Meow and Annette didn't get along. The first thing Annette would do when she walked in would be to wrinkle her nose. On her previous visit she had accompanied the nose-wrinkle with an eye-roll and a "Jeez, Mom, it smells so—catty—in here," to which Barbara had replied, "That's not what 'catty' means."

Now they left the subject of Mr. Meow alone, though they couldn't completely ignore him. He spent the duration of Annette's stay perched on the uppermost level of his cat condo, glaring down at Annette with his yellow eyes.

§

Luke Ralo had many things to worry about in his life, so it seemed peculiar that he would worry about a middle-aged white lady who was nothing to him but a customer.

She had been coming for months, first once or twice a week, then nearly every day, before he asked her name. It had been a Tuesday morning and there were no other customers in the store, so he didn't mind chatting her up.

She seemed surprised to be asked. "Mrs. Timoney," she said. "Well, that's what my students called me. My name's Barbara."

"Timoney? Timoney, really?" he said.

"Yes—"

"Such a coincidence! You see, the country I come from, it's East Timor. So funny, you have a small part of my country in your name."

"I see," she said.

He could tell she didn't see at all. Most people were not moved by the undercurrents of the universe, which, attended to and correctly interpreted, added up to a magnificence beyond words. But then, most people did not lose everything and move halfway across the world.

"Luke Ralo," he said. "That's me." He didn't extend his hand over the counter because that would have seemed too intimate.

"Nice to meet you, Mr. Ralo," she said.

He had felt obliged to object. "Please please please, call me Luke."

Now the problem of what to do about Mrs. Timoney's absence throbbed in Luke's gut. This was the kind of thing that happened on his favorite TV shows—*Law and Order: SVU, Without a Trace*. Someone disappeared and nobody noticed. Afterwards it seemed obvious that something ought to have been done.

Luke found himself thinking of her especially during slow times: late morning, after the Hispanic mothers came to buy cleaning supplies and christening gifts but before the office workers on lunch break stopped in for sticky notes and hole punches; and late afternoon, when suburbanites ordered helium balloons for weekend birthday parties. While he was going over stock lists or straightening the tools shelf, Mrs. Timoney's face would appear along with that stab of pain in his gut. But what was he supposed to do? He knew only her name and some of the long list of items she had bought. He didn't know where she lived. Could he call the police and say, I'd like to report my customer missing? Of course not. So he did nothing, and lived with the stabbing in his gut for ten entire days until she walked through the door as if she had never been gone.

§

"So, where did you go?" Luke Ralo asked as he rang up Barbara's egg slicer, placemats, and toilet tissue.

"My daughter dragged me on vacation."

"You have a daughter."

Something about the way he said it seemed accusatory. Barbara looked up at him as he filled her bag.

"Yes, I do," she said, watching for a sign that he cared one way or the other. There it was: a minute narrowing of the space between his eyebrows, a little sag to his usually cheery cheeks.

"A daughter can be a comfort," he said.

"Ha!" said Barbara. "You haven't met mine."

"Where did she take you?"

Barbara was not sure she wanted to say. But she had been so miserable for the week, had so missed her apartment, Mr. Meow, and her trips to the Dollar Bin, that she now felt the answer well up unbidden. "Coronado," she said.

"Yes, yes, yes!" Luke said in his gunfire affirmation. "I have been! The Hotel Del, that is where you stay?"

Barbara nodded.

"It is beautiful, no?"

Barbara did not know what to say. How could she explain the desolation she had felt lying awake at the far edge of the king-sized bed listening to Annette snore? That she had a daughter who snored and no husband, that the school district had given her no choice about retirement—she had asked for none of this! And to be deprived of Mr. Meow, of the props and comforts of her life—it was too much.

Luke Ralo had been the bright spot in her week away. She had thought of him as she used to think of her husband Patrick when they first dated, letting a little of him leak into her mind and warm the whole of her. She thought of Luke while at a restaurant with Annette, facing a Caesar salad composed of three spears of Romaine, five croutons, and a cross of anchovy fillets. She thought of Luke while walking beside the tufted dunes in the fog. She thought of him while brushing her teeth before the oval mirror above the chrome taps. If she hadn't known better, she would have thought Luke Ralo was her lover.

And now here he was, asking about the vacation. Instead of answering, Barbara felt her hand dart to the display of peeing cherub key chains. She plucked one from its hook and laid it on the counter while she reached again into her purse and handed Luke another dollar and eight cents. The breadth of his smile made her wish she had bought the cherub months ago.

"You surprise your daughter!" he said.

As Barbara left, the hanging bell looped over the top of the door tinkled and Luke called after her, "See you tomorrow, Mrs. Timoney."

§

Dinner was a disaster. Not the food—China Garden had come through as usual, although Annette had insisted on steamed broccoli instead of Buddha's Delight. She worried about Barbara's cholesterol. She worried too much, Annette did.

No, the disaster came after the meal, while they sat in the living room watching *Survivor*, with Mr. Meow glowering at Annette from atop his cat condo.

"These people are letting themselves be made jackasses of!" Annette said.

Barbara winced at the dangling participle. She knew the bikini-clad, bronze-skinned contestants were not real people but she liked to pretend they could have been. A few reminded her of former students.

"When I go to your house, I'll watch the shows you like," she said.

Annette rose from the couch. She made that face she always made and walked toward the window. From the corner of her eye, Barbara saw her daughter in dangerous proximity to Mr. Meow. She ought to warn Annette but at that moment the contestants began arguing about which direction to go for water. Barbara kept her eyes on the TV.

Annette's screech drowned out the argument's resolution. "Your damn cat scratched me!" She retreated to the couch, tugging her shirt down over her shoulder and twisting her head to assess the damage. Barbara pushed her glasses up and leaned toward her daughter. Two bright lines of blood ran along Annette's left shoulder blade. Barbara sighed.

"I'll get some hydrogen peroxide."

There was none in the bathroom, but she remembered buying some at the Dollar Bin recently. It would be in the hall closet.

She didn't realize Annette had been following her until she opened the closet door and heard the gasp behind her.

"Mom—what the hell?"

How must it have looked to Annette? The closet contained no coats or shoes, no hats or gloves. From floor to ceiling were stacked Dollar Bin items: baskets, bath sponges, mascara brushes, styling gel, fly swatters, cutting boards, corkscrews, boxes of spaghetti, photo holders, sunglasses, salt shakers, wrenches, glue sticks, tube socks, medicine spoons, bathtub appliqués.

"What is all this shit?"

Barbara kept her back turned. "Oh, stop with the complaining."

She knew exactly where the hydrogen peroxide would be. There it was with the other first-aid items—the no-name bandages, the cotton balls.

Annette went home after that, leaving a wad of bloodied cotton in Barbara's bathroom trash and the leftover Chinese food, improperly wrapped, in the refrigerator.

§

Luke Ralo tried to calculate Barbara's age. He began studying her face surreptitiously. It was hard to tell the ages of white women but he knew she had retired from teaching and her daughter was grown. He decided she was between 55 and 60, at most 15 years older than he.

He wished he had said more yesterday when she spoke of her daughter. But what could he say? I had a daughter. I had a wife. Enough time had passed that he could say the words. Still, when he did, it seemed another man came inside him to speak their names and recite the story. This other man painted only the broadest picture: how the dumb luck of his business put him in Dili while the Besi Merah Putih militia shot inside the church in Liquiçá. A line sliced into his life, before, after.

Really, could he speak of that among the party balloons and peeing cherubs?

A daughter is a comfort, he had said. He smiled to realize Barbara Timoney was becoming a comfort to him.

§

"I can't do this anymore," Annette said.

"Do what?" Barbara asked.

"Worry about you."

"Then don't."

"Ma, you know what I mean."

Another dinner done. This one Barbara had ordered: kung-pao shrimp, egg rolls, beef chow mein, cholesterol-be-damned. Annette's nose had wrinkled as she unpacked the cardboard containers onto the counter.

"I really don't know," Barbara said.

There were still five minutes before *Survivor*. Annette took no chances and sat at the end of the couch furthest from the cat condo. Tonight, though, there was no sign of Mr. Meow.

Annette leaned toward the coffee table and used her finger as a miniature broom to sweep dust and crumbs into a pile. "This!" she said. "This is what I'm talking about. And the hoarding."

"The what?"

"All that crap! Where do you even get it from? Every time I come over there's another bag of something in the closet. I saw you're putting stuff under your bed now."

Barbara stood up. Too fast—she felt her heart beating in that hollow space at the base of her throat, powerful enough to choke her. As if she could feel inside her mother's chest, Annette went on, "And your heart. I saw what the doctor said. Your cholesterol is through the roof. Your blood pressure is terrible."

"Heard," Barbara said. "You *heard* the doctor."

She looked away from her daughter. Where was Mr. Meow? Barbara wanted him in her arms now, the mass of his body, the engine of his purr. She walked over to the cat condo and began raking her fingers over the putty-colored carpeting covering the platform, gathering clumps of fur that had collected there. "I don't know what to say," she said.

"Listen, Ma. There's a place just a couple miles from me."

"A place?"

Annette slid forward on the couch, jittered her knee. "It's really nice. All redone. They have different levels of care, from completely independent to assisted to full medical."

Barbara squeezed her fist around the ball of fur. The action made her think of the peeing cherub. She turned from the cat condo and went to the hallway where her purse hung on the closet doorknob. She found the cherub and took it into the kitchen.

Annette was following her again.

"Ma, would you just at least listen to me?"

Barbara stood at the sink and unscrewed the cherub's head.

"I have something for you," she said. She filled the cherub's body, twisted the head back on, and turned to her daughter. "Surprise!"

§

"It's called Oak Gardens," Barbara said. "Have you ever heard such a ridiculous name? Oaks don't grow in gardens."

She stood at the counter before Luke Ralo, empty handed. She had not come as usual in the morning but in mid-afternoon and had not shopped, had not even browsed, but headed straight to the front and waited until the two kids buying ice-cream sandwiches finished counting their change and the bell on the door ceased tinkling behind them.

For the first time in a long time Luke's powers of positive thinking deserted him. He could have said, Mrs. Timoney, this means your daughter cares deeply about you. He thought about saying, It's only a bus ride away. He wanted to say, I am so sorry.

Instead he looked into her eyes. The irises were brown on the outside, green-gold on the inside, flecked like a cat's.

She turned away. "I'm going to need a cart today."

She spent more than an hour in the store. Customers came and went. Luke rang them up, all the while sensing Barbara's presence as she pushed the cart through the aisles. Her pace reminded him of how his daughter would walk when she hadn't wanted to go somewhere, the slowness of her steps an act of defiance or the chimerical dance of someone about to become a ghost.

Luke's afternoon cashier came at three to help with checkout so he could restock and get ready to close at seven. Unchained from the cash register, he went immediately to where Barbara stood in the personal care products aisle. The smell of cheap soap surrounded them. She continued standing with her forearms resting on the handle of the cart as he approached. Then she lifted a container of strawberry lotion from the shelf.

"Do you think I should get this?" she asked.

Luke reached for the lotion. He made sure to let his fingers brush hers, coffee-colored skin against peach. He made a show of reading the nonsense on the side of the container, then handed it back with a nod.

"Come," he said. "I will send Juanita to the back. I myself will check you out."

§

Mr. Meow had to go back to the shelter because pets were not allowed at Oak Gardens. But there was no prohibition against things and Barbara packed up every last Dollar Bin item. Annette was paying the movers by the box.

Once the boxes were stacked in the new apartment Annette wanted to stay and help her unpack. Barbara knew what that was all about: a chance to slip things into the trash while she wasn't looking.

She sent Annette away.

The apartment was crowded and intensely empty. It smelled of old people and dinner left out too long. Barbara sat listening for the whisper of Mr. Meow's paws and the echo of Patrick's snoring. After a while, she began to hear also the accented detonation of Mr. Luke Ralo's laugh.

▩ ▩ ▩

....

UNTITLED EROTICA

JUDY waits for Hermann in the café. She wears a wedding ring on her small, well-kept hand, but maybe she wears it as legerdemain, to misdirect the middle-aged baldies who would love to get a piece of her. She once heard an actress playing a mature woman of means explain: The wedding ring scares them off.

Judy has a perfectly good baldy of her own at home.

She sips tea and wonders how she can have taken up with a man named Hermann, a name given to rotund men past their prime, not to a man who is—she knows from the photo on his web site—youngish, with chiseled cheeks and—she imagines— an abdomen as smooth and rippled as a lake frozen mid-wave.

Of course, she hasn't *taken up* with Hermann. She hasn't even met him yet.

The trick with her mind lately is not to let it pursue a single thread. All threads lead deep into a jumbled knot of desire;

follow one too long and she'll end up inside the mess. For instance: contemplating the multiple meanings contained in the word *plot* or the fact that she has recently begun to call herself a writer. She tries to let her mind flit from thought to thought as if she were drunk, though there's nothing stronger than Earl Grey tea in the glass mug in front of her.

Judy turns her mind away from the adjectival morass that feeds the cheap pornography she has recently started writing, pseudonymously. No, not pornography. *Erotica.* She wrote the first story in an outpouring one night when Stone, *her* baldy, was out late with his law partners. God knows what started her off. Maybe her robe brushed her breasts. Maybe she felt a twinge as she crossed her flannel-clad legs in bed. She settled against the pillows, intending with all her heart and soul to edit the environmental report her client was expecting the next morning. Instead, she flipped the paper over and began writing. *From the moment she saw him across the room...* A shadow of the report's printed words showed through from the reverse side of the flimsy sheet.

The peculiar part was that she had not fed the story to the shredder. She typed it up, edited it, formatted it, and searched online for "erotica markets." Expecting nothing, as she had come to expect nothing from her many submissions over the years to literary journals, she sent it off to *Blue Iris Review*. An e-mail came back within days, accepting the story and inquiring in the next sentence if she had anything else to send. Judy felt a surge of anxiety followed by a physical thrill followed by another surge of anxiety.

Apparently there is an unquenchable appetite for the stuff. She wrote and published four more stories in the next six months.

Now she is meeting Hermann. *Her agent,* who makes her

something she has striven to be: a represented writer.

Judy has never been to this café. She doesn't make a habit of cafés. That habit belongs to Stone, who often asks her to go with him. She's accompanied him a few times but has never understood the allure. It seems a waste of time and money to pay to sit around drinking tea, which she could do for free at home. Of course Stone has his Blackberry to keep him amused. His absorption with it makes Judy feel superfluous.

Nonetheless, she likes this place. There are couches against one wall with coffee tables in front of them, like someone's living room, and the chairs have nicely padded seats that invite you to stay for longer than it takes to finish your drink.

Her Earl Grey is down to its dregs. Her watch says Hermann is five minutes late. She's not surprised. He must have other clients, other meetings.

Judy looks up when the bell jingles at the door. It's a young couple, laughing together. Eager not to look eager, she pulls out a notebook—not the electronic kind—and opens it to a folded-over page. Her handwriting trails across the paper, the same malformed letters that have dogged her since she failed penmanship in third grade. But she refuses to take the easy way out and always hand writes her first drafts. She seems to need the pen against her palm, some physical connection to that string attached to the knot inside.

Here is the skeleton of her next short story, a journey into the sub-genre of erotic historical fiction. Pablo and Maria, kept apart by their cruel employer, are finally reunited on the straw bed of the stable loft. Judy almost laughs at the absurdity of it. Real-life sex in a stable loft would be unbearable: itchy, prickly, and filled with the choking odor of the animals. Maria would be cold, or hot, or consumed with anxiety about being discovered.

Or maybe there are women whose real bodies behave just as their imagined ones do.

If Hermann doesn't come soon, she'll have to leave. Another five minutes pass as Judy stares at the last lines she has written about Maria's breasts and the blood pulsing in her loins. The thought of breasts and loins reminds her that she is expected home for dinner. Not just that: she is expected to decide on, shop for, and prepare dinner. It occurs to her that she must have somehow signed up for this obligation, but all she can think is *I didn't sign up for this*.

Will Hermann ask her to sign something?

She recognizes him the moment he enters the café. With all the imagining, she has expected to be disappointed. It takes her breath away and reddens her face when she sees Hermann is even handsomer than his photo. The photo had not shown his body but here it is, tall, lean, and muscled, garbed in jeans and a black sweater, sleeves pushed up on forearms fuzzed with red-gold hair. The first thing she thinks after lowering her head to hide her blush is how different he is from Stone, who is swarthy in all the ways his name is not.

Hermann scans the café, picks her out somehow, approaches, says her name. Judy looks up and rises from her chair. And when she feels her palm encapsulated in his grasp, she wants to swoon.

§

"I picked up a pizza!" Judy calls from the hallway. The words come out like song lyrics, a sure sign she's nervous.

Judy hopes Stone will be upstairs or in the den so he won't hear the song in her voice. But he's close by and appears before she even shuts the front door.

"Where were you?"

The corner of the pizza box points at Stone like the prow of an icebreaker.

"Meeting." She's singing again, but she can't help herself. She names her environmental client. Stone nods, perhaps distracted by hunger.

"What kind of a name is Stone?" her mother had said first off, twenty-eight years ago, when Judy started talking about him. *Strong. Dark. Powerful. When he fucks me I feel it all the way down to my toes*, Judy had wanted to say, but of course she hadn't.

She has undergone a process that seems like the reverse of sexual awakening. Lah-di-dah and chips-fall-where-they-may in her early twenties. Then pregnant, glowing, blossoming with her two children in her late twenties. Competent and motherly in her thirties. Now she is forty-nine. The children are gone and she and Stone ought to be picking up where they left off before the babies. Instead they appear to have been diverted into some other couple's life.

"I'll heat up the pizza," she says, brushing past Stone into the kitchen. "I can throw together a salad if you want."

Stone has followed her and props the heels of his hands on the island countertop. "Jude. You know I'm not supposed to have pizza."

How has she managed to forget this? His low-carb diet is not a new development. She's been cooking like a cave-woman for months now, all meat and greens.

"I'm sorry. I don't know what I was thinking."

The fact is, she hasn't been thinking. Not since Hermann slipped into the chair across from her at the café. Not since he smiled at her, all sparkly incisors and twinkly baby blues. Not since he slid his agency contract across the table. Not since he said "I want you," followed several beats later by "to sign this today, if you're willing."

Stone pats his midriff. "I'll just eat salad."

This is what happens, Judy thinks, as she pulls the pizza from the cardboard box and slips a slice into the oven for herself. It's nobody's fault. Lots of people have secret lives and get on just fine.

She tries not to fixate on Stone's chomping jaw, the cud-like crunch of the cucumber as he eats his salad. Instead she tries to think about the first time he ever kissed her and finds she cannot recall, exactly, when that was. They had jumped into bed after knowing each other only a week. He must have kissed her then, before penetrating her, but she can't remember. Perhaps that had been her mistake, putting the erotic before the romantic.

Stone disappears after dinner to catch up on some work. Judy sits staring at the seven-eighths of the pizza that's left, then dumps it into the city composting bin outside the back door. She is only slightly distressed at how much she looks forward to rejoining Maria and Pablo.

§

Judy has chosen Dominique Swayze as her pseudonym. Anything is better than Judy Barrett. She thought briefly about going back to her maiden name, but would a Moskowitz be taken seriously as an author of erotica?

The pen name caused a bit of added trouble with the contract and bought her time. She didn't sign it that day in the café. She took it home and read it as meticulously as if she were proofreading, then read it two more times. She knew she ought to have a contracts lawyer look it over, but how would she find such a person?

Hermann seems accustomed to authorial anxiety and easily changes the language to accommodate her dual identity. Judy Barrett will remain the overseeing personality. Still, she finds it thrilling that Hermann suggests Dominique create a blog.

"Start right away. You have to create your platform," he says over the phone, his voice tickling her ear. She thought Hermann would have a foreign accent but his consonants slip easily around his vowels. "Publishers like that."

"You want me to do everything at once? Start the blog and finish the book?" She has decided to expand Maria and Pablo's story into a full-length work.

"It's called building a brand."

Judy hasn't blogged before, but she's no technophobe and it doesn't seem that difficult. The funny thing is how many blogs there are about blogging. One has a handy list of steps to get started and Judy begins taking them one by one. Stone thinks she has suddenly gotten very busy with consulting. She works after dinner and on weekends in the little nook in the kitchen where she can plug in her laptop. Although Stone does his own work or watches football, being so exposed makes her nervous. The computer screen faces into the kitchen. She listens for Stone's footsteps in case he comes to get a glass of the expensive mineral water that has replaced the beer he used to drink, ready to click away from the "Meet Dominique" page she's designing.

Sometimes she visits Hermann's web site, where the photo of him gazes out, lips curved in a mild, professional smile. She's only looking for motivation, Judy tells herself, a good firm hand to keep her on task.

She's never had a password on her computer but she adds one now and names her files "Untitled," "Untitled1," and so on, just in case.

§

Judy finds herself dreaming of Charlie Silverman, the first boy she'd slept with. Why is she thinking about him now? Why is she obsessed as she never has been before with men, women, love, sex, body parts? Is it menopause? Is it the normal swell of the emotional sea that rushes in to fill the vacuum left when love recedes?

Judy had almost signed up for a radically different life. Charlie Silverman was a nice Jewish boy. She had known him since her first day of college and dated him on and off. She remembers his dark curly hair, even then thinning on top of his head but bristling elsewhere on his body, his sly laugh, the way his plush lips went slack as he slept. She'd brought him home for one disastrous Thanksgiving. The disaster was that her mother thought he was perfect.

After graduating, she'd spent six months on an internship in London and met Stone in the Victoria and Albert Museum.

Stone was a go-getter, an arranger, a man whose lips would never go slack, even in slumber. They dated for the remainder of her time in London and then, miraculously, for a year, long distance, until their engagement.

§

Stone announces at dinner one night that his work will slow down over the holidays. "I'll be home at a decent hour," he says. "We'll be able to use those symphony tickets."

Judy nods but feels her insides lurch. Has she ever really enjoyed the symphony? Has Stone? She'll have to dig in the back of her closet for her black dress. She can already feel the silk slithering against her skin, a sensation she knows some women find sensual but which Judy detests. It makes her skin crawl, makes her sweat. And the shoes—tall, pointy ones that pinch her toes and make her calves ache.

"When is the concert?" she asks. When Stone names a Sunday evening two weeks in the future Judy can't help but look at the string of days until then like the countdown to an execution.

§

In the meantime, Dominique's activities have accelerated into a whirlwind. It's all the frenzy around *Fifty Shades of Gray*. Publishers are clamoring for manuscripts. Dominique has received three offers, fielded ably by Hermann.

"You came along at just the right time," he says.

This time they're meeting at his downtown office, where she has driven on a Wednesday afternoon. By now she knows Hermann is hardly as exotic as his name might imply. He's an Iowa boy, bred from farm stock, who moved to the big city after getting a literature degree from the University of Iowa. His accent is flat and wide as a mid-western river she could dive into and float on. She doesn't say this.

"Good," she says instead. "I could use some extra cash."

Hermann sits on the loveseat with her and flips through the pages of the publishing agreements. He points to the parts of particular interest: royalty rates, foreign subsidiary rights. Judy hears these words but is focusing instead on Hermann's lips and teeth. It occurs to her that she'd like to kiss him. The desire implants itself physically in a place she had thought abandoned by such sensations and becomes the only thing she can focus on. She cannot kiss Hermann; she wants only to kiss Hermann. The impossibility of it consumes her. She watches his face and mouth like a cat watching a bug fluttering on the other side of a window.

When he recommends which agreement to sign and hands her the pen, she realizes she's ready to do anything, sign anywhere. She remembers signing the marriage license at City Hall with Stone, then practicing signing her new name, *Barrett*, so stark and straight after all the years of round and blowsy *Moskowitz*. She was one of the few of her cohort of women friends to have given up her name when she married but it seemed right at the time, part of her eagerness to assume a new identity.

"And here," Hermann says, flipping the page and pointing. "And initial here," he continues, curling his lips around the words.

§

Judy shifts her body under Stone's and tries to match the rhythm of his thrusting. She stares at the corner where an unvacuumed cobweb dangles from the ceiling, then squeezes her eyes shut and there's Hermann, grinning at her across the table in the café and reaching for her hand. Stone's exhalation explodes in her ear but Judy barely registers it.

Judy hadn't thought much about the frequency or tenor of their lovemaking until Dominique came into her life. Once every few weeks seemed just about right, as it had for years, enough of an interval so some sort of itch builds in both of them. The tenderness that follows sustains her through the day. Then they're both back to their daily preoccupations.

On this Sunday morning they lie together as usual afterwards, side by side. Once upon a time, they faced each other and held hands during their pillow talk and the words they exchanged were freighted with meaning. Now, if they talk at all, it's practical.

Judy blinks at the swaying cobweb. She *can't* talk about what she needs to do today, which is to rev up the momentum to move on to the book's next chapter. She's on a schedule now, one dictated by the publisher, so she can't wait for inspiration. In the months since she finished the outline and the first three chapters, her feeling while writing has changed. The words no longer stir arousal. Her eye is clinical. She moves and replaces words for maximum effect. She knows what must be done and she does it. Satisfaction of a different sort results.

She pushes the covers aside and slips out of bed.

"I've got some errands to do this afternoon," she says.

"That's fine with me," Stone says. "I need to go into the office for a bit." Judy finds herself relieved.

§

Here she is again in the café. She has started coming here regularly to write, instead of writing at home. She has grown to like the place even more. Usually she comes during the week while Stone is at work. She could be just another freelancer using the café as office space. The weekday waitress smiles and brings a pot of Earl Grey tea before Judy has even taken off her coat. She has come to recognize the regulars: an older couple that always shares a plate of eggs and a young man with chunky glasses who likes to set up his computer at the corner table.

At first, Judy found the conversations around her distracting. Now she finds them a soothing background to her writing and the words flow in a way they never do at home. Here at the café she doesn't have to look up and be reminded of anything about her life. It's a blank slate, this café.

This is the first time she's come on a Sunday. She doesn't know the Sunday regulars or the Sunday waitress. Her customary table is taken so she chooses the smaller one by the window where the man with the chunky glasses sits on weekdays. She orders her tea and finds herself more distracted than usual, perhaps because this table gives her a fuller view of the café and especially of the door, which rings a chime each time it swings open or closed. She opens her notebook and stares at the words.

She is working on chapter six. She hadn't anticipated how difficult it would be to construct a story beyond the first few chapters. The glorious momentum that carried her to this point—an agented author writing in a café—has evaporated like the steam rising from the spout of the teapot.

Judy puts her forehead in her palm and lets her hair fall over her face, making a tent over the page. She's hiding, a little, from the buzz of the café and the truth of the way she has begun to feel about Hermann, trying to force her mind and attention down to the narrow tunnel of words before her. She picks up her pen and puts the point to the page, right where she has left off. And because she has changed her posture in a conscious decision to restrict her view, she hardly hears the next tinkling of the bell on the door and doesn't look up to see her husband enter the café.

§

"One hundred percent honest."

Stone said that to her the second morning they spent together, in the practically non-existent kitchen of her bedsit in Kensington, knee-to-knee at the tiny table.

He took her hands in his, encompassing her in a way Charlie Silverman never had. "No secrets, no lies," Stone whispered. Judy nodded.

And so it had gone on, for years. Now, if she is one hundred percent honest with herself, Judy has to admit she's the same person she's always been: looking for something else even when she's arrived where she thought she wanted to be.

Is it lying, she wonders, if you believe it? All those "I love yous" she had sighed in the sweaty snuggle after sex, the rush she felt watching Stone with the kids when they were small, the way the two of them weathered crises like stout ships in a storm. Now she feels unmoored and upside down. Nothing is certain any more except the pull of her stories and the longing they stir.

She has been thinking about how to tell Stone about Dominique. She will, certainly, have to tell him. Hermann has already mentioned she'll need to travel, to make appearances and attend book signings. She has never shared her writing with Stone, even the earnest little stories she used to type out on her ancient Macintosh computer. He never asked. She never offered. Did that make her less than one hundred percent honest?

Judy imagines her book launch will be something like an art opening, a gala, a revelatory event. There will be a blow-up of the book's cover on poster board. She doesn't know what the cover will look like or even what the title will be. Hermann has warned her that the publishing company will handle all that and she'll have minimal input. But she is fairly certain the cover will feature a man and a woman wearing very little clothing. Dominique will approach the podium with confidence, draw the microphone toward her, and acknowledge the audience's applause with a dip of her chin. She will have chosen a juicy passage and won't mind reading it in front of perfect strangers, giving them all a thrill.

When she is done, she will look up from the page and straight into Stone's eyes.

§

In the café that Sunday, Judy finally finds her voice and begins to write, keeping her head down. Yards away, her husband approaches the to-go counter and orders two large cappuccinos, extra foam. Judy doesn't hear when the barista calls his name. She has followed the thread into her story and is deep inside her characters, mucking about as if she lived in their skins and could feel their excitement, their optimism, their belief that it would be possible to fall in love and have a fling with your agent. She doesn't hear the tinkle of the bell as Stone backs through the café door to the sidewalk, where he hands the cappuccino to a woman, much younger, who takes a sip and smiles up at him with a wisp of foam across her upper lip.

■ ■ ■

....

PEARLS

T HE house, early in the morning, is peaceful. Frank sleeps like a baffled bear under the clutch of blankets. Ingrid sits at the kitchen table and counts her irritations. As usual, she starts counting at one, since she never knows how many there will be.

One: the psoriasis that has flaked her elbows since late adolescence. It's her body's response to a kind of self-irritation, which erupts in great mottled blooms of red and white skin calling out to her, *scratch me, scratch me.*

Two: the chip in her favorite mug. Frank had whacked the mug against the granite, trying to be helpful by loading the dishwasher. Except his assistance felt not like a gesture of loving kindness but like an accusation. He might as well have said, *I'm always the one cleaning up.* She would have answered, *And I always cook.* If he thinks she should clean up too—well, that's his problem. Now, though, his carelessness has become her problem, in the form of a chip in the glaze the approximate size and shape of an incisor.

Three: the new, interior irritation that came upon her suddenly a few months ago, beginning with the sensation of being unable to swallow a mouthful of food and the occasional feeling that one of the large fish oil supplements her doctor suggested she take had lodged itself sideways in her throat. The irritation progressed to what the doctor almost gleefully labeled *reflux*. Which seems absurd because reflux has always been Frank's affliction, not hers.

Ingrid turns her gaze outward to the maple leaves trembling in the morning breeze. A crow struts across the lawn, then stops at the curb to peck at an invisible treasure. Crows are quite intelligent, she's heard. Also: they mate for life and the males cheat. What does *that* say about their intelligence? This crow is one of a group living in her neighborhood. They make good candidates for irritation number four. They settle in the tree outside her bedroom window and call to each other at ungodly hours, their rasping voices penetrating Ingrid's sleep. She complained to Frank, who shrugged and handed her a pair of ear plugs.

Across the sloping street, her neighbor's house offers irritation number five. It badly needs a paint job. Ingrid can see the patches in the tan paint revealing the ghastly eggshell blue of the previous coat. The deterioration is worst around the frame of the picture window directly facing Ingrid's house, a chafing with a result not unlike the peeling of Ingrid's skin around the elbows. If she had more energy, she would write a letter to the city. Surely there's an ordinance she could cite, a prohibition against letting a house become an eyesore. An *irritation.*

The tea has grown lukewarm. Ingrid lifts the mug with both hands and sips, avoiding the tooth-shaped chip. On the counter next to the sink is the mug Frank bought last week as a replacement, a bowl-like vessel with a handle so tiny she can barely fit two fingers through. One of those inspirational sayings is printed down the side. MAINTAIN AN ATTITUDE OF GRATITUDE. Who thinks these things up? She clinks her wedding ring against the side of her familiar, blemished mug: one, two, three, four, five.

§

She begins counting down. This time she names not her irritations but her blessings.

Five: The house across the street once contained the woman who became her best friend in the world. Thirty years ago, as a young mother stuck with a squalling baby, trying to maneuver a spoonful of baby food in to the protesting "o" of her son's mouth, Ingrid looked up from this very kitchen table and saw Elise, whom she didn't yet know was Elise, struggling down the steps with a baby in one arm and a toddler attached to the other. Though the house was a good twenty yards away, Ingrid swore she could see the irritation radiating from the woman.

Ingrid left her son in his chair—strapped in, of course!—raced to the front door, flung it open, trotted across to the far sidewalk and called, "Do you need a hand?"

To which Elise replied, "Yes, please. May I have two?"

Thus began their almost daily trips across the street. Later, there were walks down the hill to the elementary school, glasses of wine on Friday afternoons, a celebratory bottle of champagne when their first-borns went off to college and two bottles when their second-borns did. And then the treks Ingrid made during the final year with casseroles, soups, juices, anything at all that Elise might be able to keep down after the chemo, and the last trek, for the reception after the funeral.

Four: the crows. They're quite attractive, actually, with their oily blue-black feathers, a color any lady with a bit of gray would kill to have her hairdresser achieve. They deserve to live in the world as much as she does. Maybe she could learn a thing or two from the way they flock together, their dedication to one another, their in-the-moment focus on whatever they're doing—collecting bits of things, scraping road kill off the pavement with their beaks. She looks out the window again but the lawn is empty.

Three: Ingrid places her hand on the hollow beneath her breastbone, the taut skin such a vulnerable covering for what's inside. Her viscera have betrayed her: Twisting into knots, spewing excessive and unnecessary fluids. How could she possibly count such a thing as a blessing? Yet this new affliction has led to her losing a few pounds, which she has meant to do for years and never got around to, but which seems easy now because almost any food she ingests becomes an irritation. And she's cut back on the wine, shutting Frank up with his statistics about alcoholism among older women.

Frank would be pleased to hear he has assumed the number two place on her list. How did she arrive at Frank when she started with the chipped cup? Thirty-five years together is a long time, long enough so each partner's rough edges ought to be smoothed away. Instead, there's something oysterish about the two of them. Frank is a grain of sand that causes Ingrid to accrete layer upon layer of resentment. She can be grateful to the cup for serving as Frank's proxy.

The crow reappears, airborne, and swoops to perch on an impossibly tiny branch, a twig, really, atop the neighbor's birch tree. It gazes down on her with its glittering eye.

Ingrid lifts her arms from the table and scratches her elbows. The ever-present psoriasis is irritation number one. Like the regurgitated acid, it reminds her of the many ways her body can malfunction. In the inventory of human ills, these are both minor. Psoriasis never killed anyone and acid takes years to erode the esophagus to a point where she might become vulnerable to cancer. Something else will doubtless kill her before then. She runs a finger over the pebbly skin of her left elbow.

She wasn't always grateful for this affliction. The first time Frank held her naked, all those years ago, she had wanted desperately to remain clothed. He peeled her long-sleeved shirt up gently as if undressing a child. The collar stuck on her chin so she stood with her head covered for a moment as Frank worked the fabric free. He kissed her palm, her wrist, her forearm. She held her breath when he arrived at the crook of her elbow but he never faltered, kissing the smooth skin of the inside fold and then, without a blink, without hesitation, the ugly red scales on the exterior.

Ingrid finishes the last cold sip of tea. She stands for a moment at the sink. Then she unfurls a fresh tea bag into Frank's new mug and lowers the chipped one into the trash.

Outside the window, the crow lifts off from the branch, tearing the air with its raw cry.

■ ■ ■

. . . .

THE APPOINTED TIME AND PLACE

L ARA tilted Christian's chin upward so the light fell more evenly. For an underwear model, he had a lovely face.

"How's Bowser?"

He always asked about her dog, the one topic they could safely discuss.

"Great." Lara stroked blush over Christian's cheekbones.

"Did he like the toy?" Christian had presented her with a brown paper bag after last week's shoot. She'd peered inside, fearing it might be a sex toy, but it was a knobby rope tug obviously intended for Bowser.

"He destroyed it. So yeah, I guess he did."

Lara stepped back to survey her work. Her job was to concentrate on Christian's face while standing so close he could have kissed her thigh.

She was old enough to be his mother.

She nodded to indicate she was done. Christian made his way to the set: a corner designed like a 19th-century boudoir.

Lara could have watched but looking at his body, even from a distance, would be dangerous. Instead, she opened her anatomy textbook and tried to concentrate on the bones of the foot. How had she ended up with her happiness tied to an underwear model? It wasn't just the sex. She'd had plenty of that after the divorce. Somehow Christian seemed bound to Lara's reinvention of herself.

The photographer ordered Christian this way and that on the velvet couch. Lara was too far away to hear. She imagined the crisp *thwack* of the shutter eating Christian's body bite by bite. He loved to mug for the camera but never for her. With her, his face was sweet and serious and his touch as tender as a boy's, cupping his hands around a wounded chick.

Lara forced her eyes to the page. *Accessory navicular syndrome.* The precise descriptions made anomalies seem manageable. The words became a converter to transform life's chaos.

She knew how it would go. After the shoot, wearing sweatpants and a hoodie that made him look even younger, Christian would stop by the table where she was packing and slip her a scrap of paper. He'd expect her to show up at the appointed time and place because she had on five or six earlier occasions. It was a pattern, a habit, or maybe something more dangerous.

She crumpled the paper and practiced what she could never say to Christian because she didn't have his number, couldn't contact him except at photo shoots or by showing up at one of those addresses. *I've got class tonight. This has to end. It's not healthy.*

Lara crossed the concrete floor, nodding to the photographer's assistant who was vacuuming the velvet couch. Beside the door a trash bin overflowed with water bottles and empty food containers. She hadn't memorized tonight's address. She would drop the paper in the trash and that would be the end of Christian.

Lara stood for a long time beside the bin, squeezing the pulpy ball in her palm.

■ ■ ■

....

SKYPING WITH THE RABBI

J AKE'S dad drove him to Rabbi Miriam's house every Sunday through the summer and fall. The rabbi's house was twenty-five miles from where Jake and his parents lived, but his father seemed to look forward to these excursions, despite giving up sleeping late on Sunday mornings.

Jake's mother would already be sitting at the kitchen table with a third cup of coffee and a stack of work. She would look up and smile with what Jake thought of as her real-life face, un-made-up, the planes of her cheeks settling toward her mouth, the border of her lips indistinct without the usual slash of lipstick, her blue eyes floating in the naked rims of her lids. Jake wasn't so young or so oblivious that he didn't notice how fast her smile faded when she turned to his father.

"Feel like coming with us?" Jake's father would ask, as he always did. His mother would shake her head and purse her lips around her coffee cup. Jake's father would shrug, swipe his keys from the counter, and squeeze Jake's shoulder in a way that made Jake shiver.

"Okay—your loss," his father would say, and they'd head out to the car.

Jake had just been allowed to start sitting in the front seat, having achieved the milestone of five feet and a hundred pounds a few months after turning twelve. The rides to the rabbi's house gave him an opportunity to study his father's face. He noted the similarities to his own face, and, oddly, to his mother's, gravity having exerted on both his parents the same downward tug at the flesh. His father didn't shave on Sundays and Jake thought the stubble of his beard gave him a sketchy look that was kind of cool.

His father had talked a lot the first few times they rode together to the rabbi's house. This was the most time they had spent together alone since Jake was a toddler. At home their separate interests absorbed them: Jake's father down in his basement woodworking shop, Jake nominally in his room but really off somewhere in Farlands, sucked through the glowing portal of his computer screen.

"This is nice, isn't it?" Jake's father had said on the first ride. "Gives us a chance to spend time together."

The talking had petered out by the third trip, replaced by talk radio. His father seemed addicted to this kind of chatter, the host going on about some current event, railing against his conservative counterparts. Jake listened for a while and then let the radio voice become background music as he watched the office parks flash by along the interstate.

Rabbi Miriam headed no flock; no temple contained her free spirit. She taught private classes from her little house at the edge of town. A jungle of ferns grew on either side of the path from the street, as tall as Jake and reaching their creepy fronds down to tickle his neck when he wasn't looking. Inside, the house smelled of cat boxes and macaw and the gamy stench of a white rat. Rabbi Miriam kept as many animals as Noah.

Jake's mother didn't want him to be here. She had grown up secular—had never gone to temple, never observed a Jewish holiday, could never answer Jake's questions about how to pronounce a Hebrew word. But his dad had gone through it all and, with the sadistic delight of a surgeon or army general, wanted to inflict on his son the same rituals he'd had to endure.

The Rabbi Miriam situation irritated Jake. The work wasn't a problem; Jake spent less time studying than the boys who took their instruction the traditional way from the rabbi at the temple with a circle of receding hair under his *kippah* and breath that smelled like a barn in the old country. It was irritating because it was part of his parents' unconventional lifestyle, which they foisted upon Jake. For example, the ceremony and reception couldn't be at the temple because his parents didn't, they said, "buy into the whole organized religion thing." Why bother with a Bar Mitzvah in the first place if they didn't buy into it? And if the ceremony was going to be at some weird little restaurant that specialized in stuffed grape leaves, then where would the band set up? Would his parents even *hire* a band? And if they didn't hire a band, how would he ever have an excuse to put his hand on Helen Dobson's back and get close enough to smell her Herbal Essences?

§

Rabbi Miriam's rat was named Suki. At first Jake didn't go anywhere near it. But one Sunday morning the rabbi greeted

Jake and said, "Why don't you go over your Torah portion? I have to talk to Leah for a few minutes." Then she disappeared with her cell phone into the bedroom to talk to her daughter.

Jake had been over his Torah portion the night before at his father's insistence and was still upset with his father for the timing of the demand. The request had forced him away from his computer in the middle of a particularly delicate Farlands quest, during which LargeHead2 and GimmeMyCandy had been counting on Jake's superior health to withstand damage from the new attack force. Now, in defiance of the rabbi, and, in some vague way, of his father, Jake sat on the couch and left his notebook closed beside him.

Suki's cage occupied an end table next to the couch where any ordinary person would have placed a table lamp and maybe a book of photographs of the Appalachian Mountains. The rat had never shown any interest in him, but now it came to the side of the cage nearest Jake and poked its small pink nose through the mesh. The nose looked almost like a cat's nose. Jake found himself leaning toward it. The rat fastened its eyes on Jake's. The eyes were the same weird creamy blue as the marbles Jake used to collect.

Jake heard Rabbi Miriam's voice through the closed bedroom door rise high and taut the way it did when she led him in song. He extended a finger toward Suki's nose. The rat sniffed the proffered finger and then retreated to the tiny cushion at the other side of the cage, where it curled into a ball and closed its eyes.

§

The first big snowstorm of the season arrived one Saturday night in mid-November.

"You shouldn't go out in this mess," Jake's mother said to his father at breakfast. "You'll slide off the road."

"That's why we got the Jeep," his father said.

"I don't care. I'll be a wreck, sitting here worrying about you." About Jake, she meant; she never seemed to worry much about Jake's father.

Thus it was decided that, during the winter months, instead of visiting Rabbi Miriam's house, Jake would take his instruction over Skype.

§

"She can't be that old if she Skypes," said Bryan, Jake's friend and fellow Farlands quester.

Jake shrugged. "She's kind of old. Her daughter's in college."

They were stretched out on opposite ends of the couch in the family room at Bryan's house, banned from playing on the computer until three o'clock. Bryan's mom was a control freak with the computer—always worrying about Bryan's brain development. They tried to spend most of their time at Jake's, but Bryan's mom had caught on that Jake's parents left him alone to do whatever he pleased, so now she insisted that Jake come to her house where she could employ her brutal oversight. The one benefit was the food. There were always fresh chocolate chip cookies or brownies or sometimes even a red velvet cake. At Jake's house you were lucky if you got packaged Entenmann's donuts. You might even be forced to resort to Nestlé's chocolate chips straight from the bag.

"Plus she has a rat," Bryan said.

"Yeah. The rat's cool."

In the months since that first tentative sniff, Suki had grown bolder. She seemed to take an interest in Jake, so much so that during one of the last visits before the Skyping had begun, Rabbi Miriam took Suki out of her cage at the end of the lesson. The rat lay along her forearm.

"Go ahead," the rabbi said. "She likes to be petted." Jake touched the rat's back and felt the quiver of skin under the soft fur.

"What does Marmalade think about her?" Jake asked. Marmalade was the rabbi's tabby cat.

"Marmalade's sixteen. They don't pay much attention to each other," Rabbi Miriam said. "Of course I never let Suki out unless Marmalade's in the other room."

Jake's parents knocked then and Suki went back in her cage. His mother had come along that day at the rabbi's request because the Bar Mitzvah was less than six months away and they needed to talk about *plans*.

Jake let himself out the front door and sat in the chilly late fall sun on the concrete steps. He didn't want to hear their discussion. He hoped it would be quick because he wanted to be home and logged in at 4 p.m. when a Farlands update was scheduled for release. Besides, he'd already heard the worst news: the Bar Mitzvah venue was indeed to be Café Dordogne.

"It'll be nice and intimate," his mother had said. "But the maximum capacity is fifty, so you can't just invite your whole class. You have to be discriminating."

From inside, Jake heard the back and forth of his father's voice and the rabbi's. His mother wasn't saying much. It had been that way since they had first started talking seriously about his Bar Mitzvah, when he was ten.

"That's *your* thing," his mother had said to his father. "I don't know anything about it."

"Can you at least plan the reception?" his father had asked.

"Like I'm the only one who can plan a party?" His mother's voice was doing what Jake thought must be called "dripping with sarcasm." It seemed the only logical explanation for what she'd said, since she was, in fact, a party planner—she worked as the event manager for a large financial company.

That had been the first of many discussions about the Bar Mitzvah, most of which Jake had been left out of but had overheard from the sanctuary of his room. After a while he began plugging in his headphones when he played Farlands so he didn't have to listen to his parents. The *poips* and *plings* of the game's music soothed him. He especially liked the undulating roar that accompanied the extermination of a monster.

Now, on the steps in the cool air, he heard his parents talking civilly, or anyway his father was. His parents would never argue in front of the rabbi. Outside their own house they were all *united we stand*.

Jake zipped his sweatshirt and looked up at the ferns swaying over the walkway. He wondered if Suki minded running on the wheel in her cage instead of outside. Rabbi Miriam had told him she rescued Suki from a company that bred rats for experiments, so the rat was lucky to be in her cage on the coffee table in strapping good health instead of in some lab with a thousand tumors bulging under her soft white fur.

Jake's mother came out of the house and sat on the step next to him. She put her arm around his shoulder in a way that made him want to jump up but he decided to force himself to sit still because he saw, or thought he saw, a tear glistening at the corner of her eye.

§

Jake had more time on weekends to work on quests without the long Sunday drive to the rabbi's house. Since Bryan wasn't allowed on the computer until afternoon, Jake ended up playing with guys—he thought they were guys, anyway—he met online. Technically you were supposed to be thirteen to sign up for a Farlands account, but he and all his friends had started playing when they were ten, lying about their ages when they'd opened their accounts. Now Farlands thought they were young men ready to head off to college.

One Sunday morning in early December, Jake was deep into a quest with Omnivore8, chatting about tactics in the little text box at the corner of the screen. This was their final mission before they could unlock the next level. Jake lost track of time and forgot to log into Skype. His mother appeared at 10:30 with the phone pressed to her chest and a black look on her face.

"It's the rabbi," she said. "She wants to know if you're okay."

She thrust the phone toward Jake and clutched her bathrobe tighter. "Here. *You* explain what was so engrossing you had to miss half your lesson."

In contrast to his mother's pinched voice, Rabbi Miriam's was as cheery as ever. "Suki and I were wondering what you're up to," she said. "We were scheduled for a session this morning."

Jake hung his head as if the rabbi were there to see. Omnivore8 typed madly in the text box, "bro? u thr? wassup?" Jake had not yet mastered the adult skill of cupping the phone between chin and shoulder so he let Omnivore8 go unanswered.

"I—forgot." He turned away from his computer and looked out the window. Snow was falling again.

"I have another appointment this morning," the rabbi said. "Let's reschedule for later. Do you think you can remember to get on this afternoon? Four o'clock?"

"Yes!" Jake said. "I'll set my alarm."

By the time Jake turned back to Farlands, Omnivore8 had let out a stream of invective, furious at having been abandoned to battle the swamp monster alone. "a**hole!!!! that was a p*ssy move."

"srry," Jake typed, "called away." Because he couldn't exactly say he'd been talking to his rabbi.

§

Jake's parents wouldn't let him have a pet. A dog would be lonely, at home by itself all day. His mother was allergic to cats. Fish—well, what fun were fish? So when Jake chose for his *mitzvah*, the work he would do for his fourteenth year, to volunteer at the local animal shelter, his mother rolled her eyes. His father began the usual comparisons: "Why can't you do something like Henry Rostrow? He's working at the homeless shelter *for people*." But Rabbi Miriam thought Jake's choice was perfectly fine. It was about giving and compassion, she said, and never mind if the objects of that compassion were furry and four-legged.

§

Jake stared hard at the murky tunnel on his screen where Omnivore8, in the form of an armor-plated being that looked like an upright armadillo, galloped along beside Jake's own avatar, a willowy creature capable of twining itself around things and slipping unnoticed through the tiniest of cracks.

"lk out ahd," Jake typed. "arx bsts." Araxian beasts lived in little cut-outs in the tunnel walls, waiting to pounce on unsuspecting travelers.

Jake pressed his finger on the up-arrow to advance his avatar in front of Omnivore8's and then quickly hit the space bar to shoot a stream of paralyzing energy at the lurking Araxian. The creature shriveled into a puddle of blue protoplasm.

"nice shot," Omnivore8 typed.

As winter's gloom had deepened toward Chanukah and the good cheer of Christmas, the voices of Jake's parents from downstairs had grown louder. Occasionally, he could hear them even with his headphones on.

Now, in the middle of typing "thx" to Ominivore8, he heard a ringing crash followed by a tinkly splatter he thought at first was from the game. Jake lifted the pad of his right headphones away from his ear and heard his mother's shout, the single word "No!" followed by footsteps up the stairs and the slam of a door.

"weird shit here," Jake typed. "gotta go."

But by the time he logged out and took off his headphones, the house was silent.

§

The first big melt of the spring happened over a weekend in February. The sun blazed outside Jake's window one Sunday morning and made a sheen over the rabbi's face on the computer screen. Outside, snow dissolved to reveal the forms of shrubs and mailboxes.

That week, Jake's father announced they would resume the Sunday trips to the rabbi's house. His father seemed almost giddy; his mother was as taciturn as his father was excited. Jake tried out *taciturn*, a vocabulary word for the week, while observing his mother's drawn brow and scowl.

"Have a ball driving through the slush," his mother said. "And wasting all that gas."

The darkest day turned out to be March 21, the vernal equinox, Jake's actual 13th birthday and two weeks before the Bar Mitzvah. His father had offered to take Jake and a few close friends to the family's favorite steak house, a grown-up kind of place with dark wood paneled booths and red leather upholstery that Jake had first visited when he was only six.

It was Saturday night; they arrived at seven and pulled up to the waiting valet. Jake and Bryan—the one true friend who wanted to share the steak house experience—stepped out of the car and followed Jake's parents inside. They were all dressed up: the boys in khaki pants and button-down shirts with clip-on ties, Jake's dad in a suit, and Jake's mom in a swishy black dress and heels. This was his work-mom, his put-together, constructed, made-up mom, so Jake was a little shocked at the words that exploded from her in front of the hostess and the patrons lined up at the long bar to the left of the door.

"You forgot to make a reservation?" She leaned toward Jake's dad and made air quotes when she said the word *forgot*. "What the hell were you thinking? Oh, wait—you weren't."

Jake stepped back as if his mother's outburst was contagious. Lately she'd been prone to respond with emotion disproportionate to the situation. It scared Jake, as if the person who lived inside his mother's body had been replaced by someone he didn't know. Now his discomfort was magnified by the public setting and by the feeling that he would owe Bryan an explanation.

Jake's dad opened his mouth, but before he could say anything the hostess said, "Sir? Ma'am?" She scanned the list in front of her. "I'm sure we can fit you in. Let's see what kind of wait there is."

The wait, it turned out, would be nearly two hours for a table in the dining room. "But I can seat you in the lounge in a half hour."

"That's fine," Jake's father said. "The menu's the same in the lounge, right?"

"I am *not* celebrating Jake's birthday in a goddamn lounge!" his mother said.

"Thea," his dad said. The hand he put on his wife's arm was flung back.

"You do what you like. I'm waiting for the table in the dining room."

The birthday dinner stretched until nearly eleven o'clock. Jake wasn't even hungry by the time his steak arrived; he and Bryan had sated themselves on onion rings in the lounge while they waited. Why was it okay to eat appetizers in the lounge, but not dinner? His mother had sat with her coat on, using the toes of her crossed leg to fling her shoe half off her foot and back on again, periodically sliding her Blackberry out of her purse to check the time. Jake's father had tried to keep up conversation with the two boys. He asked about school and Bryan's family and, finally, mercifully, about Farlands, which was good for a whole half hour. Then a basketball game came on and the three of them turned to the muted screen and watched the players dribbling and shooting.

When the steak plates had been cleared and Jake's leftovers returned to him, wrapped in tinfoil twisted into the shape of a duck, the waiter brought Jake an enormous slice of chocolate cake with a single candle illuminating its shiny frosting. Jake's parents and Bryan sang softly.

For the first time, Jake understood how even something delicious and joyful, like eating chocolate cake on your birthday, might become merely another obligation.

§

Jake's mom wasn't up the next morning when Jake and his dad left for the rabbi's. "She's not feeling great," his dad said.

Hung over, Jake thought. He'd seen his mom ordering cocktails in the lounge, though he wasn't sure, with the distractions of the Farlands discussion and the basketball game, whether it had been two or three. He'd caught the stormy look from his father at the table when she ordered first one glass of wine and then two more during their meal.

Jake wanted it to be one of those mornings like the ones early on when his dad would leave the radio off and talk. He wanted his dad to make it easy to ask questions, even though Jake wasn't sure exactly what to ask. But as soon as they got in the car, on came the radio and the host's strident, accusatory voice blasted them for the whole ride.

Rabbi Miriam came to her door holding a shoebox and looking solemn.

"It's Suki," she said. "She's sick."

Jake stroked Suki's fur. He felt his father behind him and felt, rather than saw, the exchange between the two adults.

"What's the matter with her?" Jake asked.

"It's a respiratory infection. She's on antibiotics, but they don't seem to be helping."

"That's a shame," Jake's father said. Jake felt his father's hand on his shoulder, two taps as his father backed away toward the door. "Have a good session. I'll see you at noon."

"I think Suki might feel better if you held her on your lap," the rabbi said. "Do you mind?"

Jake sat and the rabbi gently set the rat and her cushion on his lap. Now, in the quiet of the house, Jake could hear the rough, quick rattle of Suki's breathing. She didn't wriggle under his finger as she usually did when he rubbed behind her ears.

"Is she going to be okay?" he asked.

"We'll have to see," Rabbi Miriam said.

Jake thought about Suki all day Sunday. It was amazing that such a tiny thing—the rat couldn't have weighed more than a pound—could take up so much space in his head. He even had trouble concentrating on Farlands. He let a Teruvian Brine Snake sting him and had to retreat to his home world to restore his health. Finally, he logged out and sat staring at the game's home page where a clever digital artist had arranged many of the creatures that populated Farlands—scaly, lumpy, graceful, awkward—behind fantastical trees veiled in nodding vines.

§

The morning of Jake's Bar Mitzvah held none of the anticipation of a birthday morning. It felt more like the morning of a big test and a distant cousin's wedding rolled into one. Jake's mother came into his room before the sun was up and sat on his bed. He was already awake but pretended not to be, sneaking looks at her from between quivering eyelids. He thought how much better he liked *this* mother, the un-made-up one, than the one who waltzed around the house in her fancy shoes getting ready for work or the one who scowled and sulked through a birthday dinner.

She sat for what seemed like a long time before she jostled his shoulder. "Jakie, it's time to get up. You said you wanted to take a shower, remember?"

"Mmmffff." He rolled away from her and buried his head in the pillow. "In a minute," he said. He felt the slight rebound of the mattress when she got up. Jake rolled back and saw his mother had pulled the door almost all the way closed, as she always did, so she could hear when he got up and shut it the rest of the way. He wished he had said something more to her, but he couldn't think of what.

He got out of bed, showered, and began the construction of Jake the Bar Mitzvah Boy. He pulled on the rented tuxedo pants and ruffled shirt, the black ribbed dress socks that imprinted his ankles with their cruel elastic. His mother helped him with the bow tie and the cummerbund.

"Isn't that a funny word?" she asked, fiddling with the clasp behind his back. But by this time she was his made-up mother and he didn't respond.

§

The ceremony was over. The DJ had started playing songs while the waiters passed appetizers. The songs were from the seventies and eighties, nothing Jake and his friends knew. Jake couldn't hear the music anyway; he hid in the coat check room among scratchy wool arms and slippery silk shawls, surrounded by the smell of perfume and mothballs, holding Helen's hand.

Jake had loosened his cummerbund and all the tension of the last months and weeks and days and hours seemed to have drained onto the floor of the coat check room. Never mind his parents or what they were up to. They could go ahead and *do it*, the Big D, just like some of his friends' parents had, leaving the kids dangling in the chasm rent by the divorce. *Go ahead.* Jake didn't care. All his senses now concentrated on Helen and the sweaty tingling of his palm where it touched hers. This felt better even than the thrill he got from a well-aimed shot to an Araxian beast's soft spot. The fingers of his other hand rested on a different soft spot, the place on Helen's neck where it started into the curve that became her shoulder. The spot was partly covered by her hair, which smelled of Herbal Essences.

"Jake?"

The rabbi's voice came to them muffled by the coats. Jake's hand froze. Looking into Helen's widened eyes, Jake seemed to feel an invisible energy connecting his pupils to hers. It reminded him of the beam from the headlamp his Farlands avatar wore to light the path through the Myolesian Caves.

Then Jake blinked and backed out of the line of over-garments that hid Helen.

"I was looking for my Dad's coat," he said. He prayed the rabbi wouldn't glance down to see a pair of legs and shoes that ought not to have been hanging with the coats.

The rabbi leaned on the counter in front of the coat check. Her face looked tired, like his mother's un-made-up face, and older than he remembered, with lines around her mouth and a wrinkle on her forehead between her eyes. Jake moved out from behind the counter and stood beside her.

"I can't find it," he said.

The rabbi settled her arm around Jake's shoulders. He felt the softness of her body and smelled her perfume, something sharp and rosy. She let him go. "Feel like getting some air?"

Jake gave a single, helpless glance back to the coat check and followed the rabbi out the restaurant's side door into an alley that smelled of garbage.

"This wasn't the kind of air I had in mind." Rabbi Miriam laughed. "I just wanted to say you did a beautiful job today. You're quite a young man."

The rabbi leaned against the wall of the restaurant and looked up at the darkening sky. Jake leaned back and looked up with her. A sliver of moon hung enticingly just above the roof of the building across the alley. He liked how the rabbi never seemed to say more than was necessary. His mother, for example, would have added whole paragraphs on to the rabbi's three sentences.

He heard Rabbi Miriam take a deep breath.

"I didn't want to tell you earlier," she said. "I didn't want to distract you. Suki—"

She didn't have to finish. Jake nodded, looking down at his shiny shoes sticking out from under the cuffs of his dress pants. Why did all the awful words begin with D? He was leaning against the wall but felt as if he was falling backwards. He brought his hand up to his face. His skin smelled sweet, like Helen's shampoo. Snot leaked onto his fist.

Rabbi Miriam kept to herself against the wall until Jake was ready to go back inside. Then she offered her flower-print handkerchief and Jake blew his nose in the rose-scented silk like some kind of pussy, or maybe some kind of damn hero.

.

▦ ▦ ▦

. . . .

PUT THE SWEATER ON THE DOG

T HE stupid dog yaps at everything. I get up to grab a beer, the dog yaps. I go take a piss, the dog yaps. The pizza guy comes to the door, the dog yaps. I'm sleeping in my own fucking bed and even with the pillow stuffed into my ear I hear the stupid little dog, yapping.

The yapping is a problem because technically the apartment complex doesn't allow pets. I say technically because I've seen the lady in 3A dragging a bag of cat litter up the stairs. But a dog is harder. A dog doesn't shit in a box. A dog you've got to take outside and walk around, even a little wiener like this one with a white fluffy coat that looks exactly like the hair of her previous owner, my grandma. And then there's the slobber. I know dogs sweat through their tongues but I don't want that gross saliva all over me.

It's a Tuesday morning and I'm taking the little stinker out into the alley to do her business. At least she's small. I bundle her under my coat when we go downstairs in case the super happens to be snarking around. I feel her wiggling like a live sausage next to my shirt and a strangled whimper escapes through my coat.

"Shhh, shhh, shhh," I whisper. "*Donatella.*"

What the fuck kind of a name is that for a dog? A wishful thinking name, that's what. Maria-Sophia always wanted a little girl with a name to remind her of the old country. A name to make you think of olive trees and wine. Instead she had to make do with my dad, her fuck-up of a son, and a dog now walking around with what should've been her daughter's name.

§

From the minute you're born, you're dying. So technically anytime you're looking at someone, you're watching them die. *Actually* watching is different. I was there when Maria-Sophia kicked the bucket and it isn't something I'd wish on anyone.

I called her Gamma because that was the only way I could say grandma when I started talking, and it stuck. Gamma would've rather I called her Nonna like a good Italian grandson but my mother wanted her side of the family to get some recognition. So at our house it was *Grandma* and *Daddy* and *Mom*, not *Nonna* and *Papa* and *Mama*.

Is it normal, I wonder, to be dragging your whole history behind you like a tail? I can see Mom and Daddy sitting together on the couch, laughing. I thought they were happy but that's because when you're four you think all laughing comes from being happy.

I remember Mom saying "Carly, Carly, my sweet Carly."

And then Daddy: "Don't be calling him no sissy girl's name. That's my boy, Carlo Jacobo Spano, *Junior*."

When it got to be just me and Gamma, she called me C.J., because she didn't want any reminders at all of the original Carlo.

§

Why I'm sneaking the little crapper around, I don't know. It'd be a relief to have the super make me get rid of her. Then it wouldn't be on me. And I wouldn't have to be reminded of the last thing Gamma said to me as they wheeled her out of her apartment on the stretcher. She was already hooked up to an IV. We both knew she wasn't coming back, not with the fluid around her heart. I was standing by the door and the EMTs stopped a minute like they knew something had to happen between us, probably because they'd done this thing a thousand times before. Gamma moved her hand toward her mouth. I had to lift up the oxygen mask for her so I could hear the words hiss out: "Donatella. You'll take her."

Maybe if it had been a question, I could've taken the dog to the shelter. But it wasn't. It was an order. Donatella got it, too, I swear. Because the moment I closed the door behind the EMTs, the little yapper sat down on the plastic mat just inside and gave me a look like she was auditioning for a dog-food commercial, head to the side and staring at me with those big, wet eyes.

"Okay," I said. "Fine."

§

Tuesday, we make it down to the alley and back up with nobody the wiser. It's the time I'm at work I worry about. I know she can hold her pee while I'm gone but what about the yapping?

Somehow we get through the week undetected. On Saturday I decide to give the little pisser a treat and take her to the park. It's the same park Gamma took me to when I was a kid. I haven't set foot in it for probably fifteen years. The city's torn down the monkey bars where I used to hang upside down and give Gamma a heart attack. Now it's all yellow plastic and fancy stained wood.

But the park's where I discover the dog's magical powers. I'm walking along the path with Donatella sniffing this and sniffing that, sticking her nose into whatever-the-fuck. It's not like regular walking. Start, run forward, stop, repeat. Then, on one of the stop cycles, there's this cute girl bending down in front of me.

"Oh, she's adorable!"

The admiration's mutual. Donatella's sniffing and licking and begging for her ears to get rubbed. The girl looks up at me. I think I'd like to rub *her* ears but I just smile.

"She's yours?"

"Yup."

The girl must have been running. She's in shorts and one of those athletic tee shirts and there's just a tiny bit of sweat at her hairline. She rubs Donatella's ears. *Jesus*, I think, *the dog's a fucking chick magnet*. I'm trying to decide what I can say to keep the girl there. But before I can come up with anything clever, the girl pats Donatella, stands up, and runs off down the path with a smile and a wave over her shoulder.

§

I can't say the dog's magical chick-attracting power makes up for everything else. But there's less yapping now, like she's resigned to me. And cliché number two: it's kind of nice to have someone who's glad to see me when I get home. She's still a pain, especially having to sneak her around and even more so when I discover her nice, neat coat of fur isn't natural. I realize this after I've had her for a month and she starts to look damn shaggy. Doggy eyebrows hang over her eyes so she can hardly see. I Google "Pet Groomers" and we walk over to a place on Ashton Avenue where they give her a shampoo, blow-dry, trim, and a nail-clipping. Seventy bucks later, I walk out with Donatella looking like a drowned rat.

I'm telling this story the next Monday at work and the receptionist says, "You have to get that dog a sweater."

I don't say the obvious, which is the dog had a perfectly good coat of hair before I spent a fortune getting it chopped off.

Around then I start thinking again about the girl in the park and whether Donatella could help me out with the biggest problem in my life right now. The problem I ignored while Gamma was dying and right afterward when I was cleaning out her apartment and getting used to the dog.

I'm sitting on the couch watching TV one night with Donatella curled up next to me like a sow bug with her nose under her tail. I have to admit she's pretty damn cute.

"Wanna see someone else cute?" I say. I've been doing this a lot lately: talking to the dog. Somehow it seems natural, not wacky like you'd think it would be.

I slip my wallet out of my back pocket and slide my finger into the slot behind my credit card. I ease out the picture of Jane and hold it up so Donatella can see. I'm scratching the dog's ears and she's looking at Jane staring out at me from that photo.

Jane's been staring out from the photo just that way for the last year. I don't know why I expect anything different this time. Do I think this is some crazy enchanted photograph like in Harry Potter, where pictures are a window into another world?

"I don't know what the fuck I think," I say out loud to the dog. I haven't seen Jane since three months after she gave me that picture.

I wanted to think Jane was just another one in that long line of girls who seemed so promising at first and then couldn't stick it out. Things would be nice for a while—months, or sometimes close to a year. Then it'd be, *C.J., I don't think you're really committed* or *C.J., you're holding back part of yourself.* Mostly I didn't care but I guess I did with Jane, because I still carry around her damn picture.

Donatella whines like she's just as confused as I am.

§

It's getting colder. There's frost on the sidewalks in the morning. Sometimes Donatella shivers. I think about getting her a sweater. But it still seems stupid. Besides, I don't have time for sweater shopping. They want me doing overtime at work, so now my Saturdays are just like any other day of the week and I have to leave Donatella alone another nine hour stretch.

I'm lying in bed one Sunday morning in November. It's eleven already and I've been awake for a while but I'm happy not to have to get up. I took Donatella out late last night so she can last another hour. She's in bed too, curled next to me on the pillow. Her ears go up when she hears the knocking.

"Shhhhh," I say, and shut her in the bedroom just to be safe.

Through the peephole I see the super, Mr. Parker, in his super outfit, all tan and buttoned down, with a cap on his head. I leave the chain on and crack the door open.

"Mr. Spano," he says. "Some of the residents have reported hearing a dog."

"A dog?"

"Yes, a dog."

"I don't have a dog."

"You are aware that pets are not allowed under the terms of your lease."

"Must've been the TV."

"Maybe you should turn down the volume."

"I'll do that," I say.

I hear Donatella whining as I close the door. My heart is hammering away in my chest. I bust back into the bedroom. There's Donatella looking up at me. She makes that swallowed little whimper like she knows she's done something bad. I don't want to do it but I lean down over her and start to yell in that whispery kind of way you use when you don't want anyone outside the four walls of your apartment to hear.

"You little shit! How could you be doing that? You're going to ruin everything with your stupid yapping. You should know better. What do you want, me to drop you off at the shelter? Maybe you'll find some family with a kid who pulls your tail and forgets to feed you. Or maybe no one'll take you and they'll send you off to doggie heaven."

Donatella runs to the corner and looks up at me like she thinks I'm going to hit her.

I slam my fist into my palm instead. I wasn't going to hit her. I wasn't.

"Shit," I say. I head toward her but she shimmies away under the bed, so I sit on the edge and press my palms against my skull to keep everything in—or maybe to keep everything out.

"I'm sorry," I say. A whining sound starts to come out of me like the sound Donatella was making a minute ago. "I said I'm sorry, you little crapper. Sometimes everything is just too much."

Too much to be a guy in his twenties, babysitting his dead grandma's dog and dragging his past around like it's a pit bull clamped to his calf. You'd think I was a veteran of the fucking Iraq war with PTSD or some such, given all the visions I have. Visions of the Gamma's kitchen floor where I used to crawl around all the grownup legs until I got to know the linoleum like I knew my own skin. Visions of Mom and Daddy fighting, and of Gamma pushing me behind her and me trying to peek around her thighs into their bedroom. And not just visions but sounds too, like my mother's voice when it went it went all high and tight, a scream strangled in the back of her throat.

Gamma never screamed. Even when she made me go to school. She made me go because I was *at risk* and everyone knew it. I might as well have had a big sign around my neck saying *kid of a junkie*. That's all anyone saw. That's all *I* saw when I looked in the mirror at my greasy hair hanging down over my eyes and my lips curling back over my teeth.

I feel something brush my calf. I reach down and Donatella lets me rub behind her ears. Something warm spreads in my chest like when I was a kid and I pissed inside my snowsuit.

§

Jane used to cook for me. She loved to cook. She tried making the dishes Gamma made but something was always missing, not quite right.

The night she left, Jane threw a plate of *involtini* at me. "You're in love with your fucking grandmother!" she screamed. But I wasn't. I was in love with my grandmother's *involtini* and Gamma was too sick to make it any more.

Jane brought her voice down almost to a whisper. "So go. Go back to your precious Gamma." Never mind we were in my apartment and Jane was the one grabbing up her coat and her purse, shoving her feet into her Uggs.

I covered my ears because her voice echoed just like Mom's did when she screamed at Daddy. *You're in love with your fucking crack pipe!*

Everyone is always screaming and leaving. I just want a quiet house where no one screams and no one leaves.

The pivotal day came when I was eight—old enough to know Daddy wasn't like other dads. He was in bed all day but not because he was sick. At night when other dads were in bed mine was out somewhere. "Stepping out," he called it, like he lived in some 1930s movie.

Mom went with him when things were good. But even the good times weren't. I'd stand behind Mom and watch her get ready to go out. I could see something crooked and funky about her eyes staring back at mine from the mirror and something wrong with the shape of her mouth when she drew her lipstick on.

Then one day I got home from school and Daddy was up. He was never up before five but this day he was on the couch with Gamma, and no Mom anywhere.

Gamma patted the cushion next to her. She was a big lady so I rolled into her when I sat down and got close enough to smell the Prell shampoo she used on her hair, which back then still had some black in it. She put one arm around my shoulders and pulled me even closer.

"Your mama went. She had enough of this." Gamma waved her other hand around the living room. "You'll come with me, C.J."

Daddy didn't say a word.

§

The Running Girl is there again the next time I take Donatella to the park. Only now she's bundled up in sweatpants and a sweatshirt, with a fuzzy blue headband covering her ears. She jogs in place and gestures at Donatella.

"Isn't she cold?"

I shrug. "She's a tough cookie."

Running Girl stops jogging and bends down to pet Donatella. I think the dog really likes her.

"Are you a dog person?" I ask.

Running Girl laughs. "Is that a pickup line?"

In a way it is, though not the way she thinks. I've been hatching a plan. "No, I'm curious."

"I had a dog when I was a kid. But now I work a ton of hours and I don't think it would be fair to the dog."

"But you run. The dog could run with you."

She stands up and adjusts the headband. "Gotta go before I get stiff. See you."

Donatella lunges after her as she takes off down the path.

I start going to the park more often, even after work, but I don't see Running Girl during the week. I don't let myself think that's why I'm going.

The next Saturday it's colder with that damp bite that says snow, maybe. We've been at the park a half hour already and my hands are frozen. I forgot to bring gloves because let's face it, I'm not there for the fresh air.

Finally, Running Girl jogs by. Maybe I'm imagining things but it seems like her face lights up when she sees us. Then she runs over. This time, she gives Donatella only a moment of ear rubs before she stands up and jogs in place to keep warm. She looks at me sternly.

"Put a sweater on this poor pooch! She's freezing."

On the way home I wonder why I've been so resistant to the sweater. Don't I want Donatella to be warm? A sweater is nice. A sweater is comfy cozy. You can wrap it around you and feel like the person who gave it to you is hugging you. Or if it's fucking cold out, a sweater keeps you warm. And anyone can see Donatella is shivering her ass off.

Jane would say, *You're being passive-aggressive.* That's what she used to say when she wasn't accusing me of being in love with Gamma. *You pull away and then lash out with your damn sarcasm. Can't you be honest about how you feel?*

Maybe it's the indignity of the sweater. Dogs aren't meant to wear human clothes. I don't care how cold it gets. That's the whole point of being a dog: some things you just don't need. Then I hear Jane's voice again. *Yeah, maybe in prehistoric times, but dogs these days are our little playthings. We've bred all the wild out of them so now we've got to put sweaters on them when it's cold.*

And it's true. I can feel how shivery Donatella is when I stuff her inside my coat and go into the apartment building.

Inside, I make coffee and sit at the kitchen table. Donatella noses my leg. She expects a treat when she gets back from a walk. That was Gamma's doing, always doling out food to the ones she loved. I get a Milk-Bone from the cabinet and make the dog sit for it. Then I bring up the subject that's been rattling around in my brain for weeks.

"Donatella," I begin. She looks up at me like I'm the most fascinating person in the world. "I've been thinking. You're a cute dog. I really like you. But you've got to admit, it's kinda silly, the way we've been living. Sneaking around, worrying what the neighbors are going to say."

Donatella wags her fluffy stub of a tail.

"I know your favorite person in the world isn't here anymore, that being Maria-Sophia-may-she-rest-in-peace. I know anyone else is just going to be second best. But I think there's a better second best for you out there. Someone better than me."

I stop and clear my throat. Why the fuck is it so hard to have this conversation with *a dog*?

"So I've been thinking. You know the lady at the park? The one with the headband?"

Donatella flops herself down, crosses her paws, and gives one of those wheezy dog-sighs.

"She seems like a really nice lady, don't you think? And she likes dogs. She said so." I leave out the part about the long hours she works. Because what's the difference—I work long hours, too.

"So—what do you say we propose to her next weekend?"

As soon of the words are out of my mouth I feel what I've done. It's like an explosion in my chest. Because there's a huge fucking difference between *proposing to* and *making a proposal to*, which is what I meant to say. Somehow I'm out of breath, even though I've just been sitting there.

I don't know what I expect from Donatella—tail-wagging, joyous yapping, vigorous head nodding—but she just rests her chin on her paws.

"It's up to me, is what you're saying."

I reach down and bury my fingers in the fur behind her ears. She pushes her head against my hand and turns to lick my palm. It doesn't seem gross to me anymore, just a sign of trust and contentment.

The aftermath of the explosion in my chest feels warm and comfy.

"Okay, then," I say. "Either way, we're getting you a sweater."

■ ■ ■

. . . .

SO SHE SAYS

S HE says she's having a baby.

Strange, given her age.

Stranger still, she says it's my baby.

Not possible, I say. But I'm not sure I mind. So, what are you planning to do about it?

Do? It? Are you one of those pro-choicers? She aims the question like a missile.

I guess. I hasten to add, Not if it's mine, though. If it's mine, I want it.

Oh, it's yours. She sticks my hand on her belly where it stays like a leaf on wet pavement. Or maybe the leaf is the baby: translucent, fluttery, prone to skittering away.

Did you ever—?

She's asking a question I don't want to answer. But I have to. When she said *I'm having a baby* she pulled me into that Territory of Honesty where even guys who've spent their first thirty years as good-for-nothing fuck-ups have to come clean.

Never had to make a hard choice, I say. Fuck, I've never even had a long-term *relationship.*

You might be starting one. She stands, bends left and right like she's warming up for yoga class. My back hurts, she says. It's not supposed to yet but it does.

I try again, more gently. So what're you thinking?

I'm thinking I'll go on one of those baby websites to see what they look like at twelve weeks. That's when it happened, right? After Jeremy's party.

There's no way I could know. My life's not exactly a sequence of memorable events. I can only guess Jeremy is some common acquaintance who had a party around Halloween.

Right. Jeremy's party.

Then I'll see the OB-GYN. Only she pronounces it like a word, obe-gyne, with a hard *g.* And I'll have to quit booze. And coffee.

That *is* noble.

A shrug, a smile, a reminder of why in the first place I unbuttoned her down to bare skin. I flash back to her hair like sheaves of wheat tenting my face.

I don't expect anything, she says. I just wanted you to know.

It's my turn to stutter through difficult sentences. *I think I might. I need. Would you be okay if?*

The thing is—she juts her hip out and drags the honey wheat across her shoulder—I want to do this on my own. She looks out the restaurant window where it has been raining all this time.

Suddenly, I love her. I love the baby. I've already lost her and now I'm losing the baby.

That's not fair, I say.

I'm forty-one years old. I never planned on this.

Like I did, I think but don't say.

Goodbye, she says.

She flutters across the restaurant. I could follow. But I sit my ass back down in front of the empty mugs and exhale hard enough to blow open the door she's about to leave through.

It'll be okay. I can look her up. I know her name. I've got her number.

Or so I say.

■■■

. . . .

WHEN ALL ELSE FAILS

WE didn't see much of my dad after that Christmas in 1994 when he stood outside for what seemed like hours pounding and wailing at the locked door. The pounding and wailing went on as my mother wrenched open a drawer, clanged a metal stockpot into the sink, and ran it full of water.

We knew what that meant: spaghetti. And not the kind where an old Italian *nonna* poured hours of love into handmade meatballs and sauce from scratch, but the new American kind you made because it was the fastest, easiest thing to put on the table when all else failed. If you were my mother, you would serve it when under stress, which usually meant you couldn't remember to stir while it was cooking or time it properly, so the spaghetti—Ronzoni from a cardboard box—would come out with large segments stuck together like a bundle of cable. The sauce—Ronzoni from a jar—might fall victim to uneven heating in the microwave, one spot scalding your tongue and another barely warmed. And don't forget the Kraft Parmesan cheese from a cardboard container with a white plastic built-in shaker.

The pounding and wailing stopped as we helped my mother clear the dishes, but not before we had heard some words we weren't meant to hear. Julie and CeeCee and I began making more noise than we needed to, on purpose. So we didn't notice the exact moment when the sounds outside stopped. That made it all the weirder, as if our father had dissolved like a particle in water or dwindled like the light of a dying star you barely notice until it's no longer there.

Our lives went on. I expected what would come next would be a divorce. That didn't happen. My father moved a few miles away to a cruddy apartment over a hardware store at the edge of Streetsboro. Without a divorce there was no need for child support or alimony. My father kept depositing his paychecks into the joint bank account, showing up at Cee-Cee's chorus concerts, and taking Julie out for ice cream. He thought ice cream was too childish for me, almost grown up. Instead he invited me to breakfast at the diner down the street from his apartment. I refused to go.

I was starting to understand that an outsider, and especially a daughter, might never understand what goes on between two people, especially her parents. Now I understand my father was preserving hope—hope that my mother would change her mind, that he could change, that he could continue going to concerts and plays and birthday parties as if nothing had changed, that one day we would share a cup of coffee.

My mother hung on to hope, too. They both kept that filament of hope flickering until one day a couple of years later when my father drove his big rig straight into an oncoming school bus.

It happened on December 13, 1996, midway through my sophomore year at Berkeley. Yes, it was Friday the 13th but we didn't hear about it until Monday. We never got the details. Was it a suicide attempt? Was he drunk? Was it just an accident? Oh—I see, you're thinking he died. No. He made it, but barely.

It *could* have been an accident. It happened outside Chicago at dusk on a winter's eve. A slippery road may have been involved and also jumpy shadows and winking lights. My mother knew something had happened when my father failed to show up Saturday for the Christmas concert in which Cee-Cee had a solo. By this time we were used to the politeness between them, the way my father sat next to my mother with his big shoulders hunched inward, making sure never to touch her. But we also were accustomed to having him around for these events. Sometimes he even took us to dinner afterwards.

I wasn't there. I was halfway across the country, in the middle of finals, planning to spend winter break in Berkeley to save on plane fare home and working to help with tuition for next semester. When I heard about what happened that night, I imagined my mother sitting beside the seat she had saved for my father. Maybe she leaned over to ask if Julie had heard from him. Later she called his apartment: no answer. On Monday she called the trucking company and they told her about the accident.

He never came back to Streetsboro. When the rent on his apartment had gone unpaid for a month the landlord moved his belongings into storage. When nobody had heard from him six months after that the landlord tracked down my mother to see if she wanted to take over payment for the storage facility. If not, he'd give the stuff to charity.

I was home for the summer by then and privy to my mother's rebirth. In the months after the accident she had cut her hair and lost ten pounds. She still smoked but held the cigarette now in a way that showed off her newly manicured nails. I listened to her half of the conversation with the landlord. "No, I haven't heard from him... How much a month? Forget it. Just get rid of it."

Finally, then, came the divorce. A decree formalized by the law: "Willful desertion for one year." And, for good measure, "Habitual Intemperance."

That's what frightens most, to be descended from a willful deserter.

§

Sean and I had a beautiful little wedding. That's what everyone called it: *a beautiful little wedding*. Of course it was beautiful—it was at the Mark Hopkins Hotel. And not in any old ballroom, but at The Top of the Mark with a view over San Francisco in all directions.

If we'd stuck to the tradition of the bride's family paying we'd have gotten married at City Hall with dinner at Max's afterwards. Instead I felt like Cinderella at the ball. Sean and I had made our plans curled together on the angular brown sofa in his apartment. I remember his hand coming to my mouth as I opened it to object to the cost, his fingers trapping the "but" behind my lips. Sean had beautiful fingers. I used to tease him that if he left the legal field he could make a living as a hand model. With those lovely fingers he stroked me into docility.

"The money's not an issue," he said. "I want to do this right."

I wanted to believe he was doing it up for me, for *us*—the eight-piece jazz band, the caviar appetizers, the most expensive champagne. Sean passed out twenties from the pocket of his tuxedo to make sure the reception, which had already been paid for with an astronomical check, ran smoothly.

It was a small wedding that would have been smaller if not for the show Sean wanted to stage for the law firm's senior partners. And for the junior ones swimming like frantic sperm toward the prize of senior partner. They slurped our champagne and ordered mixed drinks at our hosted bar and danced with their wives and dates on the parquet floor. They took up four of the eight dinner tables. If not for my sister Julie and her husband and two kids, we wouldn't have had enough family to fill the head table.

There were signs and portents, if you believe in such things. Like the weather. At the time we laughed at the rain that started early in the afternoon and streamed down as guests arrived. What did we expect on Valentine's Day in San Francisco? Everyone said it would make for a good story. We'd never forget our wedding day!

The rain continued as we vowed to hold each other forever close in sickness and in health. As we ascended to the Top of the Mark for cocktail hour we were afforded not a sparkling 360-degree view of the city but clusters of buildings hulking in the fog.

We made it through the honeymoon and a few months of what looked like marital bliss. I moved into Sean's rectilinear apartment—but only for a little while, Sean assured me. We were going to buy a house. I felt so grown up riding in the back of the real estate agent's cream-colored Mercedes. Like I had finally arrived. Where we arrived was at a split-level rancher on a cul-de-sac twenty minutes south of the city. We held hands as we wandered through it with the real estate agent, scowling at another couple. The competition. We got the house.

Then the changes began, or maybe I began to notice them. At first they were so subtle and gone so soon I couldn't be sure I had seen anything. An outburst here, a scowl there. His face would shift as if someone had shaken a kaleidoscope behind his eyes. His voice would sound as if something were pinching his throat. Instead of watching a movie with me, Sean would disappear into the bedroom off the kitchen he had turned into a home office.

"And he's gained weight," I told my former roomate.

"Awww," she said. "That's kind of cute."

One morning I awoke to find him still in bed at 7:30 on a weekday—Sean the go-getter, who normally rose at 5:30 to hit the gym even if he'd been at the office late the night before. I rolled toward him, not sure whether to plan breakfast or feel for a fever. He lay inert against me.

I found the Lithium kind of by accident.

§

"I'll tell you the rest when we get married," Sean had said the night he proposed. And so he had, though not with words.

I called in sick that morning and held him until he woke up.

"What's wrong, honey?" I whispered. No answer. This was the Sean of the turned back and the redirected witness. Only now we were married. Now I had rights.

When he shrugged away from me and went to take a shower, I did not sit idle. I cinched my bathrobe around my waist and headed downstairs to make breakfast.

Yes, I did open the refrigerator and take out eggs, bread, butter, and milk. Yes, I put the kettle to boil. But after that I walked the few steps into Sean's office, where I didn't go without him. Although I heard the shower running upstairs I half expected his leather chair to swivel around and he'd be facing me with his elbows resting on the chair's arms and his hands pressed together under his chin.

I hesitated before the desk. Then I became that shrewish wife of movies, sliding open desk drawers, thrusting my hands into the pockets of his abandoned jacket, and finally flipping open the leather briefcase.

I served the prescription bottle alongside his plate of French toast. He looked at me with the orange juice glass halfway to his open mouth. I watched Sean with the same detached curiosity with which I had so often observed my father. What would he do? What would happen next?

Sean set down the orange juice glass, closed his mouth, dropped his forehead to the table, and began to cry.

We made it past that bump in the road. It was more like a sinkhole, but we navigated beyond it. He returned to his therapist. He got back on the Lithium and swore he would take it every day like he was supposed to.

"No fucking around, I promise. I love you, Eve," he said, for the first and only time in the six years we were together.

Then, without discussing it, we started trying to have a baby.

§

For who I am. That's how I'd like to be remembered.

Why is it so hard to know that about anyone? Because: everyone has subterranean passages filled with the crap of childhood. We paint the exterior with a glossy coat of what we think the world wants to see but it doesn't change the inside.

There I am. *Eve Corcoran-Masterson.* My hyphenated mumbo-jumbo of a name should tell you what a mish-mash I was. I lived behind a door that looked like everyone else's. It hung on its hinges and swung inward to the touch. It might have squeaked a little, just like other people's doors. I lived in my house with my husband.

"That nice young couple two doors down," is what we were to 86-year-old Mary Crowley, who waved at us from her window. To Sean's colleagues, I was the cute wife of the up-and-coming law partner. To my colleagues, I was a manager of projects, known for *getting stuff done*, whipping people into shape—even the senior execs who didn't like to be told what to do but who often needed a swift kick disguised as a gentle nudge. A woman who moved from office to car to freeway to house where I disappeared behind my wall of stucco.

You will always fail to imagine the truth about what goes on behind the stucco or what you would see if you could look inside.

Looking in on one particular night you wouldn't have seen anything out of the ordinary. The wife is in bed when the lawyer pulls into the garage at 10:24. There's nothing unusual about that; all young lawyers work late. But something is different on this night. A whiff of something in the air, perfume the wife has never worn. The lawyer is all lawyer now, inscrutable even as he strips down and steps into the shower to wash away who he was.

The wife, in bed but not asleep, hears him begin to sing. That's the end for her. That he could be singing after what she *knows* he's done. She turns toward the night table on her side of the bed and switches on the light. She is always calm in the midst of these storms. Anyone looking in would see a placid scene because they wouldn't see the months of accumulated suspicions: the briefcase now locked, the cell phone going directly to voice mail, the hours more erratic, the lovemaking both less frequent and more frantic.

Those people on the outside wouldn't understand why, when the husband emerges from the shower, she is no longer in the bed but standing before it, where she has placed a small overnight bag packed with one of his suits, a change of underwear and socks, and the toothbrush she has snatched from the bathroom while he hummed away in the shower. They wouldn't understand what she knows in her gut, that he never truly loved her, that the words he said only once were said for himself, not for her. That the betrayal began long before the cheating.

She can't live with him for a minute longer. The only confirmation she needs that she's right about everything is the way he stands before her with the towel wrapped around his waist and says nothing, not one single solitary word, but only squeezes his eyes and makes his mouth into a line and shakes his head back and forth.

And no one would see inside this woman, *me*, where another scene plays out, a scene from years ago but fresh as yesterday, a scene from a Christmas long past. No one would hear the sounds in her head, the pounding and the moaning at the kitchen door.

Later, if anyone asks what happened between them, the lawyer's wife will shrug and say, "It wasn't working out." And because California is a no-fault divorce state, there will be no further questions. Looking out or looking in, it will all look the same—just two people who thought things would work, but they didn't.

If anyone asks, she'll tell them what comes after all else fails is another day.

■ ■ ■

. . . .

THE BOY IN THE WINDOW

H E was the kind of boy who would curl up in your lap like a kitten if given a chance, but I didn't know that then. First he was just a tan smudge in the middle of the big rectangular pane. Approaching along the opposite sidewalk I made out that he was a person, and little, and the smudge was his hair. Before him was a square object, which I took at first for a computer or TV until I got close enough to see that it was a kind of play house centered in front of the window. He stood behind it, absorbed in animating tiny figures, flying them here and there with his hands.

That first day I simply walked by. I had passed the house a dozen times but not recently and it was different now, painted the color of wheat in the pictures of Midwestern farms. In the semicircular garden at the corner someone had planted flowers that matched the house and contrasted with the purple wisteria overflowing the fence hiding the side yard. Even after I passed, the image of the boy stayed with me, his tawny head in the dark glass reflecting the cloudy morning, framed by the wheat-colored house.

That night he appeared in my dreams. I had the feeling he had been flown there by an invisible hand, one that might play with us humans as the boy had played with the tiny figures. There were things I needed to ask but in the dream he stood silent. Although his eyes turned toward me I felt he looked through me, as if, no matter where his body seemed to be, he was somewhere else. I came close, questions surging in my throat and just as quickly ebbing away. He merely looked at me. He was more than half my height and I guessed his age at six or seven. It didn't strike me in the dream but I wondered when I woke why a boy that age would have been playing with figures and a toy house instead of Legos, trading cards, marbles. As I dreamed myself close enough to see the individual strands of hair falling across his forehead the boy sat down slowly, crossing his legs, cupping his chin, and gazing at the ground in perfect imitation of Statue of a Boy Sitting and Contemplating the Ground.

The next afternoon I made certain to take that route again, although it was out of the way to get to my new job at the café. The street, like many in that neighborhood, curved through the hills, so the house remained hidden until I rounded a bend and it appeared suddenly. My heart quickened with my steps. The window gazed at me, an eye as uncomprehending as the eye of the boy in the dream. I walked as slowly as I could, delaying the moment when I would have to pass and there would be no possibility of seeing him that day, wishing I had a dog to nose the shrubbery and give me an excuse to loiter without seeming suspicious. I bent to tie my shoe although it was perfectly well tied already. When I stood, I looked once more at the window, still blank, and listened to my heartbeat. He had disappointed me again.

That day at work, and in the following days, I tried to put the boy out of my mind, but the more I tried the more insistently he appeared. I would think for a while I was making progress and then suddenly, without warning, there he would be. The image of him in the window would flash like a slide in a slide show, blotting out the task before me—tamping down espresso grounds, making change, reaching into the bakery case for a scone. It was a mini blackout. I would come to, seconds later, with the machine hissing before me or the customer's hand extended for the coins or the array of baked goods awaiting my selection. Hey girl, I heard more than once, I ain't got all day.

Not until weeks later did I think to search for his phone number. I knew the address, of course, and these days it's easy to do a search on the Internet. The idea came to me one day at work. I could hardly wait for my shift to end. The café had several computers for customers but the owners didn't like employees using them, so I decided to go to the library. It would mean I wouldn't walk by the house that day. That was okay.

I ran from the café to the library. Although I had memorized the boy's address, and surely wouldn't forget it, I repeated it to myself all the way. I went straight to the children's section, the closest place with computers, and sat on a child-sized chair. I dropped my bag, typed the code for Internet access, found the site I was looking for, and entered the address. I prepared for the inevitable message: *We're sorry. Your search returned no results.* Quite likely, the number was unlisted. Lots of people did that, especially people with children, to protect their privacy.

But there it was. *M. Boghesian, 431-9818.*

§

There had been another boy, once, and another window. That earlier boy had looked down from a window mirrored by the glare of a New Hampshire winter day. Like Bo (as I began calling this new boy, after I found the phone number), he had viewed the world from a window that seemed more metaphor than window, a glass membrane demarcating his world. Unlike Bo, he waited for me. Daily, faithful as a dog, he anticipated my return by bus and the path of my feet along Bean Road. Like a dog, he told time with his body. He didn't understand the slide of liquid numerals on the face of the digital clock but he understood 4 p.m., Nonni said. No matter where he was or what he was doing, if she were feeding him his snack or trying to show him a book or rocking him after one of his fits, he would rush to the living room window for his afternoon appointment.

Oh, how the tables were turned, then. How for granted I took his adoration. Shading my eyes as I sought his form behind the sparkle, an impossibility in the reflected light, I waved out of faith that he could see me before I mounted the fourteen flagstone steps at the side of the house. On the landing I would pause a for moment during which I could feel his anticipation mounting like an atmospheric disturbance on the other side of the door.

"Thith! Thith! Thith!" he always greeted me, throwing his body at my legs, bouncing off, airplaning around the living room dangerously close to the picture window he had just been looking through. Nonni stayed back in the kitchen doorway, letting us have our moment, leaning on her cane.

§

What I told myself was, I just want to see him up close. I just want to talk to him, once. That's all. I'm no weirdo stalker. I kept walking past the house, mornings and afternoons, to and from the café. Sometimes I saw him in the window, sometimes I didn't. The times I didn't made me sad for how I hadn't appreciated having a boy wait for me in the window when I had one.

For a while it was enough to have the possibility of calling. Like a prescription for sleeping pills that helps you sleep just because you keep it folded up in your wallet. But the weeks went on and on without change. At first I had rocked easily in the boat of my new life. I liked my job at the café because it meant walking onstage every morning without thinking about anything except the part I was playing. Keeping half my hair dyed a color between purple and red, looking for just the right studs to fill the seven holes in my left ear, the silver hoop in my eyebrow and the diamond—yes, a real diamond—in my nose. When the businessmen came in for their morning fix I could see them checking out my ass as I turned away, wondering why the ass at home didn't excite them in the same way anymore.

All the while, if they only could have known the object of my affections—how surprised they would have been to see a little blond boy, forgetting that they had been little blond boys too, once.

One day things changed. My walk home started as it always did. Nothing much going on at two-thirty in the afternoon. The neighborhood lay like a snoozing cat under the sun, shining after a morning of fog as I came up the hill. My running shoes scuffed on the pavement. I felt sweat on my neck and forehead and I wished I hadn't worn a black shirt. I passed the house, glancing quickly back at the window, and, seeing nothing, continued along up the hill. At the top, I stopped to let my breathing slow. There was shade on the other side of the street and I crossed to rest under the sycamore tree that laced the sidewalk with shadows. I leaned against the tree trunk and turned back the way I had come. From there, I saw it: a patch of the back yard of Bo's house, just visible over the roof, which I had never noticed before because I had never looked from that angle. And there, in that patch, a boy ran through a sprinkler.

He played for a good ten minutes after I began watching. I could see him only when he ran to the visible corner of the yard. Occasionally I heard a screech, ai-eee, like a bird, and once a woman's voice, calling from the part of the yard I couldn't see. I took off my sunglasses and squinted to sharpen my vision. I was still too far away to see his face as more than a straw-topped smudge.

The next day I brought binoculars. Tiny ones I had stolen from Nonni when I left. She had used them to look at birds in the back yard where she set up a feeder. Chickadees, thrushes, finches, an occasional cardinal, and the dreaded blue jay, a thief who terrorized the smaller birds. The binoculars weren't the only thing I stole, but as punishment that theft was a good one, given how much joy Nonni took from bird watching. Now they could give me a bit of joy.

Only Bo wasn't outside that day. I couldn't very well dawdle like a creep with the binoculars so I made a quick sweep from the cover of the sycamore and went on my way.

But Bo wouldn't leave me. My apartment had absorbed the day's heat and now, in late afternoon, felt like a box left in the sun on the back seat of a car. I poured a glass of water and sat at the kitchen table, sweating. The paper with the phone number on it was in my wallet. I took out my prescription for happiness,

127

unfolded it, and stared at it until the setting sun invaded the kitchen in a full frontal assault. Then I picked up the phone.

§

They were sad to see me go at the café. I'd been a reliable worker, for all my ear studs and magenta hair. I gave them a week's notice and hardly a thought.

The inside of the boy's house was grander than I had imagined. In the movies people lived this way: powder rooms and conservatories, kitchens with two sinks and staircases railed by polished banisters. By contrast, the boy's mother hardly looked as if she belonged, with her limp ponytail and frayed workout clothes. I even thought she might have been the maid until she ushered me in and said, Danny's so excited to meet you.

Me too, I said.

He's a little shy, she said, why don't you come in the kitchen for a bit? That's when I first saw the two sinks and the six-burner stove and the marble countertop that put the café's workspace to shame. I sat at the table looking into the back yard, where citrus trees hugged the fence and a play structure just like in the catalogs, with ladders and swings and ropes and dark-stained wood, occupied one whole corner. The boy's mother set a glass of iced tea in front of me but I kept staring at the yard. It was so big. I felt a tickle of a tear because my boy never got to have a yard like this.

My first sight of Bo up close did not disappoint. He was an angel, a dream boy. He stood, shyly as advertised, beside his mother's chair. He was younger than I had thought—only just four—and a good thing, too, or he would have been off to school and then where would I have been?

Danny, she said, this is Victoria. She's going to watch you so mommy can get some work done.

§

The rainy season came. *El Niño* this year, which meant days of rain sluicing down the kitchen window and no outside time for Bo, who, like a dog and like the other boy now constantly in my thoughts, grew agitated if not allowed to run each day. I told his mother she should get him an indoor trampoline like the ones I had seen in the catalogs. She recoiled as if I had suggested she buy a guillotine not a trampoline but I kept working on her. Eventually she came around and purchased the circular rubber contraption that stood six inches off the ground with a handle for the child to hold while bouncing. I didn't tell her that sometimes I bounced with him, springing up and down and launching him into a pile of pillows.

Bo was a good boy. A smart boy. That made me sad, too, for the other boy who never would understand how the world worked no matter how old he might have gotten.

The rain didn't let up, all through late April and into May when flowers ought to have been abloom. I began taking Bo outside anyway, onto the spongy grass of the back yard and for walks into the hills where rivers of runoff washed along the edges of the sidewalks. He liked to squat beside the gutter and drop leaves into the eddying water.

By then I was watching Bo every day while his mother worked in her office at the end of the house opposite the kitchen. Sometimes she would transform from maid to princess, appearing in tan linen slacks and a silk blouse with a cashmere sweater-coat and gold earrings and her hair in a bun, and announce she was going out to a meeting. Occasionally I would come on a Saturday so the boy's mother and father could have a date night. Bo and I spent those evenings snuggling in the parents' bed, watching a movie and eating forbidden chocolates.

It was during those times alone with him I began to tell the story of the other boy, the other window.

I followed him through the muddy woods, my boy, in springtime when the skunk cabbage unfurled in the marsh and snowmelt dripped from twigs stinging the backs of our necks. I had to follow close. Much as he loved the woods, he didn't understand the darkness that could swallow you up. Nonni didn't like me to take him in the woods but he loved it so. You are your brother's keeper, don't you know? she said. She waited, looking out the tiny window on the other side of the house from the boy's big window, staring past her beloved birds, waiting for us to return so she could breathe again. It was her job as a grandmother, she said, to worry.

He was like you, Bo, I said, he would run free if he could. At home, though, once he settled down, he was like a cat in my lap. Those times when the oil ran out and the house was cold Nonni built a fire using logs we dragged in from the woods and we sat with hot chocolate and the boy's head on my knee for hours. Cold? Bo asked. It's never that cold in California, I said. This was New Hampshire. New Hamsher? he said.

But he wasn't like you, Bo, because you can talk sentences and he never could. Even though he was twice as old as you. And he couldn't use the potty. And sometimes we had to help him eat. Bo laughed then, about a boy eight years old who needed help to eat.

Sometimes, snuggled in the bed, I closed my eyes and felt Bo's head on my shoulder or his sharp little elbow in my ribs

130

and it was not Bo I was feeling, but the other one. I kept my eyes closed a long time, knowing when I opened them there would be the fire and Nonni and the hot chocolate mugs grown cold.

The more I talked to Bo about my boy the more I felt the rest of my life emptying around me like water sucked down a drain. I still went home to sleep every night but my apartment was grayed out, dimmed into the background. What was real and alive was Bo's house, coming around the corner every morning to see it as I had first seen it almost a year ago, wheat-colored in the fog. What was real was Bo's body rushing to me as I entered, almost like the other little boy body, and his mother's smile as she adjusted the scarf around her throat before she stepped out. Even the father, seen only glancingly, coming downstairs on a Saturday evening in his going-out-to-dinner clothes, seemed to vibrate with a life I felt nowhere else. If I slept as late as I could on Sundays, the one day I didn't see Bo, then I would have only a little while in my apartment until the library opened and I could sit in one of the comfy chairs on the second floor among the fiction with a book open on my lap, waiting for Monday.

Summer came again and Bo started going outside to play. There was an unusual hot spell in late June and I arrived one Monday morning to find a pool in the back yard, twelve feet across and four feet high, with a filter so you could leave the water in it. His mother said, We set it up yesterday and Danny loves it. Of course you always need to be out there with him.

Of course, I whispered, of course.

That afternoon I felt as old as Nonni. I wished I had a cane to lean my burden on. All Bo wanted was to play in the water. I pulled a lawn chair right up next to the pool and stared at him until my eyes ached from the sun glancing off the water and my clothes were soaked from his splashing. I calculated the distance from the edge of the pool to the center, how long it would take me to reach in. I wondered how his mother could have agreed to this.

A few afternoons passed with Bo splashing and me staring and I began to relax, just a bit. I heard Nonni's voice, This is your penance, my girl, she said.

§

I only went inside for a second, to answer the phone. I was watching him the whole time. It was his mother on the phone wanting me to find an address in her home office. I looked out the window and there he was, jumping like a salmon, spraying arcs of water in the air and screeching ai-eee, ai-eee. I set the phone down on the kitchen table. Bo was jumping. My boy had been jumping too, through the crunchy New Hamsher leaves. I only bent down for a second, to tie my shoe. I heard him screeching, ai-eee, ai-eee. I looked one more time on my way to the office and there he was, jumping and jumping. I glanced up from my shoe and there he was. The office was dark with the blinds drawn against the heat. I found the address book with its cover like the leathery leaves of the forest around my feet. Back in the kitchen, the phone fell from my hand. Ai-eee, ai-eee, I heard at the edge of the river, and then nothing. Back in the kitchen, the window framed the silent yard and the tan smudge in the still pool.

***

· ·

PUDDING

RIANNA stares at the pudding. The surface stares back like one of the cow pies she and her brother used to avoid, running through the fields. Who eats pudding anymore? Old people like her grandmother, that's who.

There's the spoon beside it, shining dully under the hospital fluorescent. There's the napkin, cradling the spoon on the putty-colored tray, and her hand, inert in her lap.

"I—" she says, managing only that single croaked syllable as if the pudding were already clogging her esophagus.

"I know you don't want to, honey," the nurse says.

Brianna cements her lips together.

"You're making great progress. Up two pounds this week."

She knows. She feels the pounds added to her body by the liquid concoction they're pumping into her day and night through the IV, watched over by the nurses to make sure she doesn't rip it out. Everyone will be so happy she's gotten to this stage. Putting the food in her mouth herself. She can hear her mother's voice. *Brianna ate? She ate some pudding!* She feels the pudding polluting her pure body, every added pound dragging her down from the realm of pure spirit to which she aspires.

Last time she ate anything resembling a meal was a year ago at her grandmother's. Her brother and grandmother sat across the table, her parents on either side. Her exposed plate shouted her bodily weakness to everyone: the chicken with its wrinkly brown skin, bathed in its own melted fat; the baked potato split down the middle and upholding a mound of sour cream as white as the zinc oxide ointment her brother spread on his nose before working his lifeguard job. There was nowhere to hide. So Brianna ate.

She looks down again at her hand emerging from the fuzzy cuff of her bathrobe, at the blue veins, the bruised flesh around the IV insertion.

The card her grandmother sent stands between two vases of flowers on the window sill. Brianna almost threw up when she opened the envelope and saw the card's image of a plump grandmother holding a little girl's hand. Now she's grown used to it. The hand-holding mesmerizes her. That two people can engage in such an act without concern for the exhausting weight of love. Inside, her grandmother wrote only three words and an initial: *Miss you. Love, G.*

The nurse takes her pulse, fingers warm against Brianna's wrist. She straightens the vases of flowers. When she reaches up to adjust the blinds, the pendulums of flesh emerging from the sleeves of her scrubs quiver, like Brianna's grandmother's. Finally, she sits in the vinyl covered chair across from the bed and shuts her eyes.

"I'm taking a little snooze," the nurse says with her eyes still closed. "I expect that pudding to be gone when I wake up."

Brianna flutters one finger, then another, then lifts the hand, finally, and closes it around the stem of the spoon.

■ ■ ■

. . . .

MISTRESS MINE

I WATCH her for a while from a distance. Boy, she looks good, legs pumping and arms swinging. She's in better shape than she used to be. She's done three miles already, almost all the way around Lake Merritt, and she's running like she just started.

Trotting closer, still hidden, I see her auburn ponytail sway above those canted shoulder blades, sweat spreading on the gray Spandex bra. It's all I can do to keep from running right up to her. But my plan calls for a period of observation. I've watched her for three days. She's running a lot. Six miles the first day, then three, probably four today. Maybe she's training for a race. Good for her.

She's rounding the curve of Bellevue Ave. and heading toward her parked car. I want to see her when she stops. If I hurry, I can beat her back. I take off sure-footed and quick through the trees at the edge of Children's Fairy Land. The breeze I generate by running presses my ears back. I race across the grass through someone's game of catch, slowing as I reach the angled parking spots. Now I try to walk sedately, as if I know where I'm going, until I pick out the white Volvo.

I sit down on the grass a few yards from the car. I watch her come towards me, breathing hard. She slips a finger under the elastic waistband of her shorts and snaps it. Tiny sweat droplets fly. I can smell her now and I think I must be in heaven, watching her liquid movements, her glistening skin, and breathing in the musk of her sweat, which I had always liked but never knew could be so all-encompassingly and piquantly *her*.

§

She doesn't show up at the lake the next day, or the next, so Saturday morning I head over to her house. I stay out of sight. Finally she comes out wearing sweat pants cut off at the thigh and one of my old tank tops. Instead of driving to the lake she takes off from the house, up into the Oakland hills.

I give her a half mile. Then I appear, as if from nowhere, trotting a few yards ahead of her. I look back and see her stiffen slightly when she notices me. *Good reaction*, I think. I pause to sniff some shrubs. She passes me and glances back, relaxed. Apparently I appear friendly. I trot beside her.

After a minute she says, "Hey, where'd you come from? Go on home."

I continue running alongside her. We come to an intersection. "Hey!" she says. "Be careful." I wait with her at the curb while a car passes. "You're a smart one, aren't you?"

She talks to me on and off. Little nothings, but how sweet they sound. I am not prepared for how this makes me feel. It's all I can do to keep from jumping on her. I form her name in my mind: *Diana*. A whine issues from my throat. "Whatsa matter, pup?" I shake all over, race ahead of her. This is going to be a whole lot harder than I thought.

§

She didn't run at all for a month after the funeral. I found this out later, listening at the window while she talked to a friend. November had been a bleak and miserable month for her, she said, and not only because of the weather.

In November, I was just a little thing. But already I knew I wasn't like the rest of the litter. I was *myself*, the same Jimmy Mills I had been until lifestyle, personality, and cholesterol got the better of me one fine late October day and put me, at the absurd age of 37, in the ICU. The same Jimmy who stared at his wife's face through a whitish fog, unable to move, unable to speak, listening to the doctors' incantations, until I lost consciousness. The same Jimmy who drifted back to consciousness nuzzled up against something warm and comforting, with four other bodies wriggling around me and a nipple conveniently near my mouth.

Those first months were confusing and exhilarating. I never believed in much of anything, religiously speaking. Certainly not what had apparently happened: *Reincarnation*. The substantiation of my spirit in the body of a German Shepherd mutt puppy. What was I to make of this? A successful businessman, reincarnated as a mute, cute, furry, four-legged creature? With nothing more to do than eat, chase balls, and receive house-training lessons, I had plenty of time to reflect. But there was nothing to make of my situation. It was simply the way things were.

The other dogs I encountered, including my own "mother" and my litter-mates, seemed to be just that: dogs. I could no more communicate with them as a fellow canine than I could as a human. I had always surrounded myself with people—advisors, acquaintances, associates, friends, and of course Diana. Now there was only myself. I was lonely.

After a few months the family began talking about "finding good homes" for me and my litter-mates. I had realized by then that I lived only a mile from my old house. Diana was often on my mind. We'd been married for five years and I'm sure I had my failings as a husband. But she was my mate. *Forever*, we had vowed, not understanding exactly how long that was. I became fixated on the idea of seeing her.

The ad read: "Good tempered, adorable puppies, Shepherd mix, great with kids, housebroken. Free to good home." I didn't wait for the phone calls. I took off. I'm sure the family didn't look too hard for me.

I learned to scavenge. Of course, I had an advantage over most dogs. I knew the good restaurants and I understood enough about human nature to know when to beg for a handout and when to wait until the kitchen help went inside so I could overturn the trash bins.

I saw Diana for the first time on the Fourth of July. Yes, it took me that long to work up my nerve, to actually go to the house and wait in the tangle of ivy by the fence until she came out, holding a platter. Her parents and sister had come down from San Rafael for a barbecue. At first I was upset by how good she looked, how normal. How could she laugh, and turn the chicken on the grill, and slurp her gin and tonic without me? But after the family left I watched her walk up the porch steps as if she were listening to music nobody else could hear. She sat on the porch swing we had hung, imagining starlit evenings snuggled together, and sobbed for a good five minutes. I sobbed with her, as best I could.

§

Now it's August. After revealing my presence on Saturday, I'm eager to accompany her again, but she doesn't run on Sunday. Monday evening is warm, promising a dusk almost like those of Diana's childhood back east. I know she loves evenings like this. Sure enough, she goes inside after work, emerges a half hour later dressed to run, and heads toward the hills again.

This time I follow her from the start. "You again!" she says. I think she's pleased but also worried about the responsibility. We pass several people walking their dogs. I pause for some half-hearted sniffs, for effect. "It's not my dog!" she says. "It's been following me." But she talks to me, telling me to mind the traffic, to wait for her at the intersections.

She does five miles and arrives back at the house just as it's getting dark. She walks up the porch steps and turns to look at me. I stare up at her, ashamed of my lolling tongue, the dripping saliva. "Poor baby," she says. "You must be thirsty." She wipes her face with the hem of her tee shirt. "But I don't want you making this your home! I can't take care of you. Shoo! Go on. Don't you have a home?" I stay where I am, panting. "Oh, all right! Just a little water."

She disappears inside and returns in a few minutes with a metal pie tin I recognize as the one we used to store dirty sponges under the sink. I want to cry, *It's me, it's Jim, give me a real bowl!* But I just dip my head and lap gratefully. She has washed the pan. The water tastes clean. I drink all of it. "Now go on home!" she says. She takes the pan back inside and shuts and locks the door.

I trot behind the hedge where she won't see me and I can sleep the night.

I don't sleep much, thinking about her and me and what I want. Questions haunt me. Why have I been put in this body? She doesn't even like dogs. She's a cat person; we had two. *Have* two. I rest my chin on my paws. Is this karma? What failing or inadequacy was responsible for this? Did I work too hard, too long? Not love her enough? It seemed, then, that we had all the time in the world. There was always tomorrow—to make love, think about having children, do this or that—until there wasn't.

I curl up with my nose tucked beneath my tail. Sleep comes near dawn, when the street lights snap off and the world is cool and grey in anticipation of another morning.

§

Next evening, I wait again for her to return. I have decided what I want. I want her to adopt me. Somehow, if I am living with her, I will be able to communicate. Her heart will open to me. I will be able to let her know she's not alone, that I didn't intend to leave her so soon, that I didn't mean to destroy our life by having a heart attack.

She sees me as soon as she pulls into the driveway. She gets out of the car slowly. She wears her beige linen suit and a black blouse, and a single strand of pearls. "What are *you* doing here?" she calls. The pearls sway on her neck as she approaches. I give a little yelp. "You silly dog." She comes up the steps. I smell her perfume. To my canine nose it is painfully strong but I drink it in. My face is level with the middle of her thighs. I think she is going to touch me.

At the pressure of her hand on my head I nose her knee. "Hey, don't slobber all over me!" But how can I help it? "Are you trying to come inside? Well you can't. The kitties wouldn't like it." She touches my head again, rubbing behind my ears. It sends a shiver down my spine to my tail, which begins wagging. "I'll bet you're hungry. But why'd you pick me, huh? Can you tell I'm lonely?"

I wag harder at that.

"You stay," she says, pointing at me. "I'll go get you something."

She returns with the same pie tin, this time filled with cat food. "It's all I have." Cat food! But it smells delicious to me now. I begin to eat. "I shouldn't be doing this," she says. "I can't take care of a dog. Maybe I can find you a good home."

She sits on the top step and goes on talking as if to herself. She talks about my death. I stop eating and pad close to where she sits, lower myself next to her. "I guess I'm still grieving," she says. She twists the pearls around her neck so tightly the flesh bulges. "I tried to be strong. I thought if I just went on with my life..." She releases the pearls; they unwind and slither into her blouse.

I dare to move closer. I lift my chin and rest it on her thigh. Bliss. I close my eyes, feeling the warmth of her leg through the sparse fur under my chin. I try not to pant and drool, but it's impossible. The air is warm; I must cool off. She doesn't seem to mind.

"I've been going to this grief group," she says. "It kind of helps." She strokes my head, running her fingers from my eyebrows back behind my ears, again and again. I remember the

142

way she used to massage my neck when I was tired. I feel the same love in her fingers now. Or am I imagining things?

She gets up suddenly. "Gotta go, doggie. I've got a group meeting tonight. What am I going to call you? I can't keep calling you 'doggie.' But if I give you a name..." Her voice trails off as she goes inside. I know what she is thinking. Naming implies intimacy, responsibility, sentiment. If she names me, I will become, somehow, *hers*. I hear her climb the stairs and move around in the bedroom. I whine as she comes out the door and walks to the car. She looks back and shakes her head. "What *is* it, you silly pup?"

I am saying *name me, name me, name me!*

§

I'm waiting when she returns from her meeting. She stops and pets me before she goes in. "All right! I found a solution. A home for you. One of the guys in the group has a daughter who's been wanting a puppy."

This is not going the way I planned. Curse this body! If I were a cat, she would open the door and welcome me in. I trot down the steps to the sidewalk. Can I tell her, merely by my actions, that I don't want to be with some silly motherless girl, I want to be with *her*? But she doesn't get it. She calls after me, "They're coming this weekend, so you stick around!" And she goes inside.

That night, I debate my options. I could disappear. But when I reappear, Diana will call the widower and off I'll go. But if I stay, I'll be taken this weekend for sure. "How cute!" the little girl will say. I can feel her tightening the collar around my neck.

I trot down the block, filled with restless energy, wanting to *do something*, to act, or perhaps simply to howl. Instead I wander all night and most of the following day, returning to our house in the evening just in time to accompany her on her run.

§

She feeds me after the run, and rubs my ears. Then she says, "I've got company tonight. Gotta go get dinner started."

An hour later a silver BMW pulls into the driveway behind our Volvo. A man gets out. He carries flowers in a paper cone. It hits me suddenly: he is here to have dinner with my wife. I look him up and down. Curly brown hair. White shirt, khaki slacks, those silly boating shoes. I dislike him instantly. I hang back in the bushes, wondering whether to rush out and pee on his leg. But I leave him alone. She must have seen *something* in him. He rings the doorbell. I glimpse her in the doorway, framed in the light from the hall, like a silhouette in a dream. She is so beautiful. Will he revere that beauty?

I lie on the porch and listen through the open dining room window. I hear silverware clicking on dishes. I smell ratatouille. I love her ratatouille. Jealousy rises in my doggy throat. They're eating by candlelight. They drink a lot of wine. I glean from the conversation that this is practically a blind date; this guy Ken's sister attends the grief support group.

They retire to the living room. I hear music, Chris Isak's *Wicked Game*, one of her favorites. We had often made love while listening to it. I raise myself on my hind legs, paws on the windowsill, trying to see into the living room. It's no use. When the music ends I hear her voice, quite distinct. "We should go someplace more comfortable."

"Like where did you have in mind?"

She doesn't answer, but I hear footsteps, and I know they are headed up the stairs. I can't believe this is happening. My wife is going "someplace more comfortable" with this man. *She's going to bed with him!* Rage coils in my limbs. I trot back and forth across the porch. They are up there now. She is turning down the sheets on our bed, *where we slept together*. I have been dead less that a year and she is inviting this man into our bed!

I hear the bedroom window open above me. Oh, do I have to *listen* to them, too? I can't stand it! I begin to bark. I bark and bark. My bark comes out rough and growly. It's satisfying to make this loud, grating, annoying noise. I bark solidly for a minute before I hear him say, "What the hell is *that*?"

"It's a stray dog. I'm sort of keeping him around until the weekend."

"Can't you quiet him down?"

"I don't know what's gotten into him. He's not usually like this."

"At least close the window." And I hear the window clap shut.

But this is worse! Now I *know* he is kissing her. I imagine him pulling off her shirt and pawing her beautiful breasts. I want to die again. I want to sink back into the mist that crept around me just before my heart stopped. Then I remember. Only an old, flimsy screen covers the dining room window. I know, because I meant to fix it, along with so many other things in the house, and never got around to it.

I press my nose against the screen. It resists. I am going to have to use my claws. I balance with one paw on the window sill and scratch at the mesh. It tears easily. I poke my head into the hole, enlarging it as I wiggle my front paws and shoulders through, then drag my back legs behind me and jump to the floor. I'm in!

I waste no time. I trot upstairs, cursing the clicking of my toenails against the hardwood. Down the hall to the bedroom, dark but for a candle on the nightstand. He is propped on one elbow, lying beside her on the bed. They are both naked. Their panting drowns out my own. They don't see me standing at the door. His hand is on her just as I imagined. I pause. I feel power building in my legs like an itch. I know I can leap across the room and land on top of him. I crouch. I spring.

Diana screams as she sees me leaping, but he never knows what hits him. He rolls off the bed and I jump on his chest. He looks up at me. The terror in his eyes pleases me. I lower my head to bite his neck. I don't think I will kill him, just scare him a little. I clamp my jaw on his shoulder. It surprises me, how soft his flesh feels. He squirms, trying to get at me with his fists.

"Ken! Ken!" Diana cries. I hear her open the nightstand drawer. I taste Ken's blood, a good, metallic taste, better than I would have thought. I want to take a chunk from him and swallow it, but I'm afraid if I let go he'll get away. I hang on, growling.

I look up at Diana on the bed. She is kneeling with her arms outstretched, pointing something at me. She is magnificent. Then I remember. "If anything ever happens to me," I told her, "if you're ever alone, get some protection. I know it goes against your principles, but you never know what might happen."

It's a tiny thing, a .25 probably, but it looks enormous to me. My jaw goes slack. Ken rolls away. I stand with my silly tongue hanging out. "Crazy dog!" she sobs. "Crazy thing, I *liked* you!" And then I hear the bang and see the flash. Before the world goes white I have just enough time to pray, and I pray *please, God, next time let me be a cat.*

■■■

. . . .

BAD LUCK WITH CATS

A POTENTIAL catastrophe—the kitten strangling to death in the tassels of the afghan—pales beside what happens years after the near-strangulation when Margaret trips over the same now-grown cat.

The cat's vocal cords were damaged by a respiratory infection in kittenhood. Without her hearing aid, Margaret does not notice the breathy chirrup that passes for his meow. Without her glasses, she cannot see the wraith swirling at her feet.

Margaret falters like a fledgling at the stairhead. She wears a robe chafed so thin it reveals the folds of flesh at her elbows. The belt is cinched near her breasts, which, like south-loving birds who travel in one direction only, migrate lower each year. Her mind tells her hand to reach for the banister. In earlier days this might have saved her. Now the impulse slows to a wavering thrust that prevents her hand from grasping anything but air.

Her mind takes a lazy spin as her body spreads and then contracts. What parades through Margaret's thoughts are not her dead husband or faraway sons but the three successive felines who turned her from a dog person to a cat person.

Her friend Donna, a Francophile, named the first—Frenchie—and passed him on to Margaret when she moved.

"They don't take cats," Donna said, the way she might have said, "They don't take credit cards."

"But Timber—" Margaret began, referring to her German Shepherd.

Donna waved her hand with the assurance of a Parisienne.

Frenchie survived another eighteen years, unburdened by the absurdity of his name, outliving both Timber and Timber's replacement.

Frenchie had never encountered this particular set of stairs; Margaret and James moved into the house only after the boys were grown and Frenchie was dead. A hundred times each day, Margaret had traveled up and down the stairs when James was sick. Plates and medications went up. Soiled sheets and the letters James wrote came down. The letters ceased when the tumor embraced the optic nerve.

Finally, their son Trevor said, "Let's move Dad into the guest room and I'll stay upstairs. It's easier for me to walk up when I visit than for you to do it every day."

Trevor the younger, the practical, the dutiful. Was it ever so? All children mold themselves into their expected forms.

After James, Margaret moved back upstairs and didn't miss having a dog. But she missed the presence of another heart beating within the walls of the house—even a heart the size of a plum.

Having begun life with dogs—who learn the sounds of the syllables with which they are called and reprimanded—Margaret never thought to change the names of the cats who came to her. Buttercup, an abandoned purebred Burmese, arrived from the shelter already in her dotage and lasted only two years.

The cat in question, the third and final, precipitator of the misstep, is, fittingly, all black. He came to her as Blackie, and Blackie he remains.

"I worry about you on those stairs, Ma," Trevor said.

"Don't worry about *me*," she said.

They never tell you in which direction your life will flash before you—from beginning to end, or in reverse. Halfway down, Margaret is a young mother. James Junior and Trevor are driving her crazy, chasing Frenchie and pulling his tail. When it all becomes too much, Margaret puts herself in a time-out and sits in the bathroom on the closed toilet with Frenchie in her lap.

Backwards must be the direction because now she is marrying James; now, on their first date, she takes matters into her own hands and kisses him; now she moves into the inconceivable time that is like the present when he is not part of her life.

At the age of nine, Margaret fell from a horse. She takes the fall again now, a lithe girl with pale silk hair fanning as she descends, only a few feet, onto soft grass. She is shaken and bruised but without lasting injury. Her golden retriever runs to her across the field.

And before that? The film winds down; your mind cannot hold memories made before you have words.

The spindles of the banister look like trees along the roadside, making strobes of the shadows as she passes. These are straight stairs with no midway landing to catch her. The final resting place will be the hall in front of the door where Trevor will nearly stumble over the body. He will cry out and make a gate of his arm to keep his brother from entering behind him.

Plunging along with Margaret, Blackie squeaks.

■ ■ ■

....

DOSED

TREVOR McLain lies straitjacketed beneath the sheet of his childhood bed.

He was once so full of hope it threatened to bubble out of his nose like laughing milk. He had felt something amazing was about to begin. Now he's merely tired, having been through this cycle before, more than once, more than twice—too many times to count the way things wheel past from birth to death with barely a pause. Hope now seems ridiculous, like a virus or a cockroach or one of those fungi that live frozen underground for eons before springing to life at the dawn of the next interglacial period. Who can manage hope as the earth warms to unsustainable levels?

Hope seems out of place considering that his mother has just fallen down the stairs and died.

Trevor stares at the ceiling. He hadn't spent much time with his mother lately but her absence makes a smudge in his psyche as if she'd been rubbed out with a dirty eraser. Trevor used to hate the deceptiveness of that hard nubbin at the end of his school pencil, how it looked functional and yet when you stroked it over the offending letter it powdered off, spreading a shadow of graphite.

Today there will be a funeral. Trevor has made the arrangements because he always arranges such things. His brother Jimmy is useless despite being three years older. Half the time Jimmy is stoned and the other half nobody knows where he is.

The clock's numerals slither from 8:01 to 8:02. NPR feeds Trevor the news in soothing cereal-sized bites. But here is the dark smudge again, which he managed to forget momentarily while thinking about Jimmy and the irrationality of hope.

He must get out of bed because people are counting on him. People are always counting on him: his wife, Fiona, and his daughters, Dee and Allyson. He wonders whether they need him or only his archetype as provider of earthly goods and arbiter of squabbles. His employer counts on him, and the newspaper carrier to whom he mails cash each Christmas. One hundred dollars is many times the suggested tip, but he can afford it and she seems just this side of destitute, driving through his well-constructed neighborhood in a model of station wagon that hasn't been manufactured in twenty years.

His mother had counted on him, too, especially since his dad died. He'd kept her household running, though he isn't the handiest of men. He'd snaked the drain, shoveled the driveway, and called in experts when a job was beyond him. Now the house asks nothing of him.

Fiona doesn't like him staying here. "It's morbid," she says, "sleeping in the house where your mom died." But driving back and forth every day when there are so many arrangements to make seems wasteful and tiresome.

Now he begins to think Fiona may be right.

"Five more minutes," Trevor says aloud. His voice echoes off the room's walls, which his mother had stripped of his posters and decorated with framed watercolor prints. He hears a thump and a patter. He tenses his body under the sheet. The patter comes into the room, jumps on the bed, and begins kneading his chest. It's Blackie, his mother's cat.

A large enough dose of hope might whiten the smudge of death until it disappears altogether. Nothing can save his mother and nothing can save him from having nearly tripped over her body at the foot of the stairs. Those things are over and done with. Now there is only the clock and the cat and the startlingly foreshortened string of moments that stretch before him until his own end.

Blackie's claws prick Trevor's skin. The man sits and the animal slides to his lap. Purring begins. Trevor has never much liked cats but the deep rumble radiating from the warm labile body soothes him. He reaches a hand from beneath the sheet and rubs his knuckles under the cat's chin.

From here, seated in bed with the sheet bunched around the cat in his lap, there's not much effort required to slide his feet to the floor. Trevor swivels his body and sends the black cat darting across the room. His mother had long ago removed the hooked rug that sat beside the bed during his childhood; touching the cold floorboards is a shock. Still, the encounter of Trevor's feet with the floor sparks a crystallization of will.

Someone intends him to get up.

It comes as a surprise to Trevor that the person who holds this intention is himself. Trevor straightens his knees and stands.

■ ■ ■

. . . .

THIS AIN'T NO FAIRY TALE

1. ONCE UPON A TIME

O
NCE, not so long ago, a poor little boy named DeShawn lived in a part of the city where danger lurked around every corner.

The brown bricks of the house he shared with his mother and younger brother rose like stacks of shit toward the pallid sky, which DeShawn never saw much because he tried not to go outside. When he did venture out, he looked over his shoulder for danger, not upward to the secrets contained in the heavens.

Nobody cared whether DeShawn lived or died, except maybe his mother. Crystal Williams clung to the scaffold of her work like a woman floating in the wake of a shipwreck. She donned a plastic hairnet each morning to serve meals to the students at the elementary school where she had insisted DeShawn, and then his younger brother Taye, spend their days.

Now DeShawn was galloping away from her, a stoop-shouldered, sullen-eyed high-school freshman. She didn't see how she was going to get him back.

Elsewhere, in the city's haven of green lawns and houses like palaces, lived a woman named Lisa Arendsen whose children had grown up uneventfully and left for even greener lawns. When she heard about DeShawn and Crystal Williams, her heart fractured into a million shards of grief. The pieces flowed through her body and infected her with a restless angst she hadn't known since her youth.

Lisa could not imagine how she might ever meet a boy named DeShawn; her children were named Richard and Arthur. Yet when DeShawn's voice came through her radio, she could picture him in his kitchen and herself beside him at the cracked Formica tabletop.

Lisa could not evict DeShawn and Crystal from her mind. One morning, as she drank coffee at the kitchen island she had designed with her husband, Lisa laid her forehead against the granite. She wished for the cold stone to burn through her frontal bone and suck out the fragments of pain. But it did not. She raised her head. A shaft of light struck her through the window along with the revelation that she must act.

2. TALKING

Everyone was arguing about gun violence because a bunch of white kids got shot at a school in another city. DeShawn had seen kids get shot, though not at school. And the shooter wasn't a nut job and nobody from the TV news came to talk to him about it. A shooting was just the next thing that happened one evening while you stood around on the porch with your friends.

What the social worker at school didn't get was that you had to walk on that porch every day, right over the spot where the person's insides had come out.

The social worker said, "DeShawn, I know you have some feeling about what happened. Why you keeping that all inside?"

DeShawn shrugged. Inside was where everything had to stay.

DeShawn's mother, Crystal, stayed inside except for walking to and from her job at the school, or when she needed to go down to the Avenue for food. Sometimes she sat by the window with the curtain pulled back just enough to see the kids outside. Maybe if she kept watching she could protect them. Shoot rays from her eyes, put a force field around them like on that Star Trek show. While she looked, she ran her fingers over the skin inside her forearm and felt the striation of scars.

Sometimes the social worker came to the house and talked to her. Crystal, like her son, didn't think talking did any good, but Miss Kendra Jackson believed in the power of words. When the radio station had called looking for someone to interview after the shooting at the white school in the far-off city, she volunteered herself.

Miss Kendra came from the same part of the city as Crystal. She had empathy and an understanding of how things were. Miss Kendra, however, had gone down a different street, one that led to a diploma framed on the wall. She could have moved on to green lawns and big houses but she returned to her roots.

Crystal was surprised every time Miss Kendra knocked. Who would come back to this place if they didn't have to?

Crystal made Miss Kendra a cup of her magic brew. Really it was just coffee, but Crystal had found an enchanted solace in it now that her veins were clear of harsher poison.

"I worry about DeShawn," Miss Kendra said.

"He ain't been sleeping good," Crystal said.

Miss Kendra nodded. "I try to talk to him at school but he don't say much."

"Sounds like DeShawn."

The women shook their heads over lives filled with wayward boys.

3. MY BUBBELEH

Lisa's first-born son burst from her womb testing her patience and her devotion to motherhood. Richard's button eyes and Sephardic curls hardly compensated for his cunning ways. He used to spy on her through the bars of his crib with a wicked grin before slipping away like smoke through a grate, causing Lisa anguished minutes of searching until he rematerialized in another room. He continued the testing right up until he came home from a year of hitchhiking and announced he would apply to college after all, having consumed her energy and the best years of her early middle age.

When Lisa heard DeShawn and Crystal's story on the radio, she wondered how she could have worried so intensely about whether or not Richard practiced his trumpet, how frequently he cleaned his room, or if he got a B or a C in algebra. He had a trumpet. He had a room. He walked to school along a route unobstructed by an army of angry young men.

How had *she* ended up as the one chosen not to suffer?

Lisa's white-haired *bubbe* had spoken only once of Lisa's great-aunt. Bubbie gripped Lisa's hand with fingers that seemed almost without flesh. Lisa felt the cold feather of her grandmother's breath on her cheek as Bubbie whispered "Deborah." *Gone to Buchenwald in the back of a cattle car.*

Lisa's *bubbeleh* escaped while her great aunt and uncle and their two children were incinerated.

"Why didn't they take you, Bubbie?"

"I was out buying *broyt*."

So Lisa's fate had turned on whose turn it was to buy the bread.

Now she was guilty simply of being alive, although she had not asked for it and had not chosen this life. But after fifty-seven years trespassing upon the planet, surely she could not be expected to renounce her privileged place.

Long ago, she had attempted renunciation. She'd had relations with a tall, dashiki-clad professor. She had unbuttoned his sleek skin and swum inside his foreign body. Yet when the time came to unite herself for life, Lisa chose as her counterpart someone who might have been her mirror image: Ira Arendsen, an escapee from the same horrors Lisa's grandmother had fled.

They were the latest in a long line of survivors and yet DeShawn was not her son; Crystal was not her sister.

4. SISTERS

Miss Kendra Jackson had a sister once who was swept away in the muddy water of the drainage ditch behind their childhood home on Jamaica Street. When Miss Kendra strayed too far, her sister's ghost called her back, which explained why she had returned from the ivy turrets of higher learning.

Now she spent her days in an office the size of a crypt. Most of the time the space bristled with boys and girls with nowhere else to go. Miss Kendra made a nest of her office where she fed the children love, and words. In rare moments alone she pressed her fingers into her ears to keep her sister out.

She made DeShawn her special case. Something about the boy's laugh, rare though it was, put Miss Kendra in mind of her ghostly sister, who now laughed with the abandon of the dead.

5. KINGDOM'S END

By early spring, the shards of Lisa's heart had reassembled into a multi-colored inspirational banner such as might wave at the head of a parade. She had no choice but to follow.

Lisa set out from her house on the kind of afternoon usually reserved for working in her garden. A warm wind blew. The ciphers of new life swelled from the earth: tulips, robins, bees.

That first day, Lisa drove just to the edge of the strange kingdom and sat in her car. The asphalt was more rutted and the houses wearier than on Lisa's street, but otherwise the neighborhood seemed ordinary. Two men talked on the corner. A woman pushed a baby stroller.

The next day, Lisa drove by DeShawn's house. She knew it was his because Bubbie had whispered the address in her matter-of-fact and ever-helpful way.

The day after that, Lisa parked.

6. CREATURES OF HABIT

In April, DeShawn stopped going to school. Miss Kendra went to see Crystal again. When Crystal heard DeShawn was not where he was supposed to be, she pulled DeShawn's younger brother Taye by his arm into the kitchen and sat him down. He looked at the floor to escape the laser beam of his mother's eyes. All Crystal could see was the way the fuzz was starting on Taye's upper lip the way it had on DeShawn's a few years before. They both looked like their father when she first

159

met him, before his habit ate him up. She almost didn't have the heart to yell at Taye but she knew she had to drag out of him whatever he knew.

"Crystal," Miss Kendra said after the mother's words stopped echoing around the room. "Let the boy alone. He don't know about his brother."

7. AMBUSHED

DeShawn finished with school the day after the radio reporter came to interview Miss Kendra and DeShawn walked into an ambush in her office.

"This is DeShawn Williams," Miss Kendra had said. "DeShawn, you mind talking to Ms. Fleming from WFRT?"

Caught like a fool with his jaw down he said stuff he shouldn't have. Then he couldn't take back his words and he was mad—at himself, at Miss Kendra, at the world in general. He was mad at his English teacher, who gave them that fucking fairy tale to read the first week of school. Some crap about princes and princesses turning themselves into birds and whales, a nasty stepmother poisoning the king. There was plenty of mean stuff in the story but in the end they all lived happily *and made all their people happy too*. That stuck in DeShawn's mind. The idea that happiness could spread from person to person.

The next day he walked past school and kept going to the abandoned apartment complex. Everyone knew that's where you went for the things you weren't supposed to have. It began to rain as DeShawn approached the cluster of three-story buildings. He stepped through the peeled-back chain-link and up to the first building, which was once an office. The door gaped and he walked through, just to get dry.

"Double-you fart?"

That became the joke with Mauricio, Yusef, and P-Man. They cracked up at the name of the radio station. He didn't mind. They knew, without him having to say, about the shame of running his mouth to the reporter.

They were older than DeShawn and hadn't been to school in years. They lived here and there and then here again, scrambling through alleys and over fences, appearing like gremlins when you least expected them. They were not motherless. Each had come from some woman's womb but the women who bore them had long since dissolved into their pasts.

P-Man was their leader. P-Man wasn't his real name, but you learned as soon as you met him not to ask what the name meant or where it came from. He looked out from under dreads that had seen better days with eyes that had seen too much.

8. ORPHAN

You would have to consider DeShawn an orphan now, lost to his mother the moment he crossed the threshold of the abandoned building. That didn't stop her from acting like his mother. She still loved him because he was her son. He came home every few days. She sent him off with satchels of food but they spoke even less to each other. Crystal got by, thinking, *he's only fifteen, only ninth grade.* Still plenty of time to turn things around.

9. APEX OF LIGHT

Lisa kept the car windows closed and the doors locked. This gave the streets around DeShawn's house an underwater soundlessness. As she drove, she sweated in a manner unladylike and unbecoming a fairy godmother.

She wondered how some people could so easily bridge the abyss. Social workers, for example. They must get some kind of special training that allowed them to open their mouths and produce words that made sense to the strangers across the void. Lisa opened her mouth and out came French, or the Yiddish her *bubbe* whispered to her. Nothing DeShawn or Crystal would understand.

At home, at night, Lisa read books and blogs with messages from the far-off lands she drove through during the day. Violence was always a hot topic, and privilege. What the lazy poor were entitled to, or not. Resentment distilled into anger on the message boards: "You don't have a damn clue. Nothing is going to help yo white bread a$$."

The afternoons lengthened toward an apex of light. Daily, Lisa nosed her chariot along the streets to DeShawn's neighborhood. She observed the school disgorging students at dismissal time. They paraded down the middle of the street, just as she'd heard about on the radio program, to avoid a sidewalk ambush.

One day a boy slouched toward her car and paused outside the window. His face hid in the shadow of his sweatshirt hood. Lisa could see only the glint of an eye-white and the gleam of saliva on a lip. A force flowed from the boy through the glass separating them. She searched for his eyes, making her own eyes wide and loving, to show him she was good. The hood's oval swallowed the light around it. The sweatshirt might have hidden anything—a handgun, an automatic rifle, a scythe.

The boy's power extended to the ability to stop time, which hung suspended between them until he walked away.

10. THORNY

Yusef got to be the thorn in DeShawn's side. He kept trying to get DeShawn to tell them what he'd said on the radio station.

"You talk about your mother? Your sister? What you done to your sister?"

"I don't got a sister," DeShawn said.

It sounded like fooling around but DeShawn didn't like the kid. He didn't like his questions or the way he hid in the shadow of his sweatshirt hood. The more Yusef asked, the tighter DeShawn clamped his mouth shut, the way Crystal did when she got mad.

Yusef grinned and showed his row of straight white teeth. Staring at them was like looking into a shark's mouth even though the teeth didn't have points.

Everything would be okay if he could stay out of Yusef's way, but that wasn't going to happen.

The weed they smoked made DeShawn's legs long and rubbery and made Yusef's mouth expand to fill his whole head. The days stitched themselves together with the nights. It didn't matter if DeShawn didn't go home to sleep. So many people filled Mauricio's house that nobody noticed one extra. DeShawn slept on the floor between Mauricio's bed and his younger sister's. One night he opened his eyes and saw the sister sitting up in bed. Her elbows rose alongside her head and her hands were busy twisting her hair into a knot. DeShawn noticed her breasts pushing up against her T-shirt, the nipples pointed straight at him. He would have liked to rise up and place his hands on her—not even on her breasts, maybe just on the dip that anchored her neck to her shoulder. He opened his mouth to whisper to her. But his unworthiness silenced him.

Yusef's taunting had spread its bitterness even to the part of him that had once been good.

11. MAY DAY

The first of May, the day Lisa opened the door of her car, was a hot one. Even the WFRT weatherman said so as her chariot sailed the long blocks down into the trenches. She stationed herself further from the school, across from an abandoned apartment complex where four boys had taken up residence.

Only in a fairy tale would Lisa leave the car.

When she had begun following the dictates of her heart she had ceased coloring her hair. The dark ends flowed past her shoulders; the new growth encircled her scalp like a gray cap. She had changed her attire, too. Now she adorned herself in bright cloth like a Gypsy.

Lisa floated from the car through the hot air. If she could float, then handguns and acrimony could float. Deborah and her family could float, into the sky, out of the back of a cattle car.

The hole in the chain link had grown so she did not need to enlarge it to pass through, but a prong yanked her translucent scarf from her neck. More obstacles for her dainty godmotherly feet: heaved asphalt, splintered glass. The blitzed buildings before her wept shreds of tarpaper.

For the first time since hearing DeShawn's story, Lisa felt whole and strong.

There was no door to open. She mounted three steps leading to the rectangular shadow where the door would have been, a shadow as unknowable as the shadow of the boy's face outside her car. She stood on the threshold and sniffed. The smell of something rotten seeped from the interior. A scuffling, as of rats, mixed with the whisper of the hot wind that flapped the tarpaper.

In a fairy tale, the poor little boy's act would absolve him. In a fairy tale, Lisa would kneel and breathe life into Yusef's corpse. In a fairy tale, she would be able to save not just one pitiful jokester but also the object of her attention, her fairy godson DeShawn.

■■■

. . . .

IF ONLY YOU WEREN'T SO

Y OU would have heard what I said if you weren't being so hysterical."

Anton's words felt like a slap.

"Let's start again," Gina said.

Her husband's hackles settled an inch or two and the air around him lost a few amperes of electricity. His graying hair, flirting with his collar, seemed to relax as well. "What I *said* was, they need us to sign some paperwork before they let him come home."

Him was their son, the optimistically named Anton Junior. Long before his upcoming seventeenth birthday he had dropped his first name in favor of his middle, given in honor of his grandfather Robert, and shortened it to Rob. What his parents called him indicated their opposing attitudes. His father referred to him as Anton, or, more often, simply *him*, while Gina, whose maternal love seemed big enough to encompass any rebuke, went along with the boy's self-selected moniker.

"Okay," she said. "Let's make an appointment and get it done."

§

The residential treatment center was two hours away. Anton and Gina spoke no more than ten sentences for the entirety of the drive, but Gina carried on a familiar conversation with herself, recounting her failures as a mother and a wife, attempting self-compassion, and remarking with a mixture of awe and sadness how a relationship taxes the soul in equal proportion to the joy it yields.

§

Rob appeared across the day room as if from nowhere, plumper than she remembered. He stared everywhere except at them and rubbed together the large hands he had inherited from his carpenter grandfather along with his assumed name.

"Honey," she said. Rob moved closer slowly, a wary animal.

Gina's eyes burned with the vinegar of repressed tears. She felt Anton beside her and fancied she could hear his breathing, a muffled creak of anger. Why had her husband even come? Would this visit end as the last one had, with Rob skulking through the kitchen at two a.m. after sneaking out to party with his old gang and Anton's words hurled after him, *if only you weren't so, then we could, why can't you?* And would Gina alone drive Rob back to Hill Hollow?

Gina stood, preempting Anton, and strode toward Rob. Nothing, she felt would stop her. Not the false cheer of the treatment center's silk flower arrangements, nor the yellow paint splashed like fake sunshine over walls that must absorb or reflect outpourings of pain and grief, nor fear of relapse, nor even Anton's severe and punishing attitude toward the only offspring he was ever likely to have.

"Honey," Gina said again, and went to hold her son.

....

THE BUREAU OF LOST EARRINGS

SOMETIMES the earrings catch on her clothes as she undresses. Sometimes they work themselves out over the course of hours and slip soundlessly onto her shoulder or a carpeted floor.

She wears only the dangly kinds with curves of wire that slide into the tiny perforations in her earlobes. The losses aren't frequent. But by the time Hilary's sixtieth birthday approaches, her jewelry box—though perhaps that's too generous a term for the wooden container that once held exotic tea—is home to a sizeable collection of mateless earrings.

1. COMBAT

Hilary was sixteen when she and Tanya Shoenberg took the T into Boston one spring afternoon. They walked into a hole-in-the-wall place at the edge of the Combat Zone where the owner would pierce your ears for the price of a pair of earrings. He looked them up and down. He probably thought they were prostitutes, notwithstanding their ordinary suburban clothes, because why else would a couple of teenage girls be down on this part of Washington Street? This was 1974, the year the Combat Zone received its official designation as Boston's adult entertainment district.

The piercer was almost as old as Hilary's dad. His hair hung past his shoulders and a peace sign flashed at the open neck of his shirt. They had nothing to fear from him, Hilary thought, although she also thought maybe they were being a little naïve.

Somehow she had been elected to go first. Her palms began to sweat when the guy came out with the piercing gun. That's what he called it. Then he added, It's better than the needle. Cleaner, nicer alignment. You'll be happy, you'll see. Just leave the starter studs in for six weeks so the holes won't close up.

He said all this while swabbing Hilary's lobes with alcohol and marking the spots with a pen.

Okay now, the man said, just hold still.

There was the shock of the pop and the pinch and it was over.

The only set of studs Hilary ever owned was that starter set. As soon as she took them out she went to the Chestnut Hill Mall and bought herself a pair of silver teardrops with a fake green gem glistening in the ovate center of each drop.

2. TEARDROP

She lost and found one of the teardrops twice before losing it for good in the sheets of Johnson Perkins III's bed. He was her first serious boyfriend. J.J. shared the bottom floor of a house in the Back Bay with three other B.U. students where Hilary spent almost every weekend. She was still in high school but there wasn't a thing her parents wanted to do about it.

"Tanya's having a study group at her house so I'll just stay over," she said on her way out. Or "I'm meeting Tanya at the library." They were happy to believe her. They had their own messes: a marriage on the rocks and a thirteen-year-old boy who was nothing but trouble.

She loved J.J., who was called by his initials because Johnson was too sissy a name, and he loved her. At least that's what it felt like when he burrowed under his red satin sheets and ate her out or took her to The Rat to hear Third Rail or sat with his arm around her on the gross couch in the living room while his roommates sucked on a bong shaped like a naked woman. It felt like he loved her right up until his graduation when, instead of inviting her to dinner with his parents, he told her she'd have to be sure to be *outta here*, meaning the house, before Friday night when said parents arrived. And, he added, maybe it would be better if we don't see each other anymore.

She very nearly threw the remaining teardrop earring into a sewer drain at the corner of Marlborough Street and Mass. Ave. on her way home.

3. TWO TURTLE DOVES

Hilary's mom bought her the nesting turtle dove earrings the year she graduated college. By then, Noah had been an inpatient at McLean for more than a year. Hilary visited her brother every few months but their mother hadn't seen him since the day they dropped him off.

Of course I love him, her mother had said as they pulled away.

Of course you do, Hilary had answered, without taking her eyes off the road.

Her mother handed her the tiny box at breakfast the morning Hilary arrived back at her mom's apartment, a dismal way station while she looked for her own place.

Just a little something I thought you might like, her mother said, aligning her butter knife with her spoon.

Each silver turtle dove perched on its nest of red glass. Why red nests, Hilary could never figure. Maybe because silver and red were festive holiday colors. More mysterious was her mother's thinking. Turtle doves conjured Christmas and, good secular Jews that they were, they exchanged gifts around the Christ-child's birthday with a heavy sense of irony. But this was the middle of June.

Thanks, Ma, Hilary said, and threaded the wires through her ears.

Her mother smiled and reached under her chair.

And this, she said.

She handed Hilary a box covered with silver filigree of a most hideous gaudiness, flowers and vines twining around each other, interrupted by small nests where silver birds perched. Suddenly, the turtle doves made sense.

Your grandmother kept her jewelry in it. Maybe you can find a use for it.

4. MENAGERIE

The turtle doves, founding members of an earring menagerie ten years in the making that included snakes, cats, monkeys, butterflies, and even horses, hung on until Noah's funeral.

Hilary hadn't worn the turtle doves in a long time but she remembered them as she packed the black silk blouse and pleated wool skirt, remembered the shy pride her mother had taken in presenting them along with the eggs and bacon that morning.

Were the turtle doves too festive for such a somber occasion? Hilary studied herself in the steamed mirror of her mother's bathroom on the morning of the funeral. She decided no. Her brother wouldn't mind a little festivity.

On the plane home after the funeral she supported her elbow on the armrest and leaned her head against her hand. She stared out the scratched porthole. Cold air trickled up from the crevice between armrest and window. The plane seemed in a hurry to return her to the two little girls and the husband waiting in Albuquerque. Hilary's fingers ached to tickle her girls' chubby bellies and comb themselves through the feathery silk of their hair. Combing her own hair as if in preparation, watching the Midwest unroll below the plane, she felt the absence of the right-side turtle dove.

Reflexively she checked her left ear. The other dove remained, a singleton now.

5. DOUBLES

The first time her husband bought her jewelry they'd already been married for ten years. He had a good excuse: cash flow. There had always seemed to be something more important to buy for birthdays and anniversaries, like a new washing machine or replacement roof tiles.

Doug the engineer was so proud of himself when he handed her the two indistinguishable boxes, both embossed with the name of a fancy jewelry store. Hilary opened one to reveal gold rectangles etched with her initials. She opened the second and found identical gold rectangles bearing identical initials.

Now it won't be a big deal if you lose one, Doug said. You've got backup. He plucked an earring from one of the boxes and held it to her ear.

Hilary covered his hand with her own and guided it back down to the table. For a moment, they both stared at the hunk of gold that fairly screamed *expensive* and *suburban matron.*

Thank you, was all she could think of to say. How could someone who had shared her bed and her life for ten years choose a style of jewelry so utterly at odds with who she was? She'd have to lose three of the earrings to put both pairs out of commission.

6. STUDLY

If one were having an affair with a married man, it probably would be best not to wear earrings at all. What if one snagged on your lover's sleeve and he accidentally brought it home and incriminated himself?

Probably it also was best not to give a gift of earrings to your lover, but Hilary couldn't stop herself. Matthew was eight years younger than she and wore an adorable diamond stud. She loved to lick around it and bite his lobe playfully as if to chew off the gem. When they had been sneaking around for six months she presented him with a single emerald the same shape as his diamond but more raucous and demanding of attention. She could tell the minute he opened the box that he'd find some excuse not to wear it.

When Matthew broke off the affair, he gave her back the emerald stud. I'm sure you could use the money, he said.

Who the fuck was he to know whether she and Doug needed money, even if they did have one college tuition to pay and another on the way? She laid the stud to rest with the turtle

174

dove, the four gold initialed rectangles, and a lonesome horse, the last surviving member of the menagerie.

7. ALL IS LOST

To be accurate, not everything was lost. The moving company mislaid only two of fifty-three boxes, one containing kitchen utensils and the other containing Hilary's collection of scarves and her grandmother's jewelry box. She was unsure which loss was more upsetting: the box or the earrings it had contained.

Look at it this way, Tanya said. Now you get to start over.

Who wants to start over at forty-nine? Hilary whined.

She and Tanya Shoenberg had rediscovered each other when Hilary moved back to Boston after her divorce became final. Now the house in Albuquerque was sold, the proceeds divided, and Hilary felt just like her mother.

Tanya said nothing but a few days later presented her with an empty tea box.

To start your new collection, she said, and handed Hilary a second, smaller box. Inside was another pair of earrings. Red orbs hung from gold chains like fat pinpoints of blood.

Red jade is the stone of life-force energy, Tanya read from the slip of paper folded inside the box. Wear it to overcome the fear that holds you back.

Hilary removed from her ears the only pair of earrings that hadn't been lost in the move because she had been wearing them, an utterly ordinary pair of department store silver hoops, and replaced them with Tanya's gift. The weight of the jade tugged at her earlobes, which she had noticed recently were slackening along with the rest of her skin. The bloody orbs swung merrily on their gold chains and tapped her neck when she moved her head.

She wore the earrings non-stop from that moment until the day, four years later, when she graduated from nursing school.

8. ADDICTION

You need different expectations when you change careers in your early fifties, Hilary said to Clem, her first serious boyfriend since the divorce. She still couldn't believe it—*boyfriend, serious*—at her age, which would be fifty-five in a few months. Contrary to popular wisdom, the mirror did seem to lie. She hadn't looked so vibrant in years.

Clem was a pharmacist at the hospital and he wasn't even fifty yet.

I seem to have a thing for younger men, she'd confided to Tanya.

She'd had to assure Clem after a few dates that she was no Nurse Jackie; she was already divorced and certainly wasn't a pill-popper like the tragic fictional nurse on the hit TV show.

Everybody's addicted to something, Clem had said.

Earrings. For me, it's earrings.

Clem must not have believed her because he never bought her any. That was fine with Hilary, who found that men's ideas of what jewelry she should own always missed the mark. When she landed the job at Brigham and Women's, she went on an earring-buying spree. She quickly began losing them, like expensive new sunglasses that disappear days after you buy them.

9. CURLICUE

Tanya caught divorce from Hilary like a contagious disease with a long incubation period. Luckily it happened after Hilary finished nursing school. She'd had no time for anyone but herself during those years of mad studying among kids half her age. But the timing was still lousy, because Tanya needed a place to stay and Clem had just asked Hilary to cohabitate. That's what Clem called it when he popped the question, grinning behind his salt-and-pepper beard.

Hilary suspected several of her earrings had succumbed to the sandpaper ministrations of that beard. One morning, noticing the absence of one of her favorites, a simple twist of silver with a delicate curlicue at the end, she began turning upside down every location in her apartment where he had nuzzled her, starting at the kitchen counter—unfolding and examining each page of the *Globe*, holding up the dish towels by their corners—and moving to the living room, denuding the couch of its cushions and conducting a grid-patterned search of the rug.

Clem was at work but Hilary had the day off. She yanked the sheets from the bed—still her bed, still her apartment, not yet officially cohabited. She shook the sheets, listening for the tell-tale plink of metal on hardwood. Then the pillows. Then she got down on her hands and knees and sighted under the bed across an expanse of floor that could have used a vacuuming. She ran her hand between the headboard and the mattress.

Goddamnit, she said to no one, wondering why this loss was annoying her so much.

She and Tanya and Clem were all grownups. They ought to be able to work something out. Instead Hilary felt like she was sixteen again, cradling her friend's emotions in one hand while

177

stroking her boyfriend's ego with the other. It was ridiculous, the way you lived the long arc of a life expecting to come to some pinnacle of wisdom and found yourself trudging up the same slopes again and again. She thought of Tanya, who no longer looked like the Tanya who'd accompanied her to the Combat Zone all those years ago, soon to be out on her own and, if you were being honest, seeming much worse for wear than Hilary did. Poor Tanya. Poor Clem. Such a sweet bear of a man. But was he the bear she wanted to spend the rest of her life with? Because that's what this would mean, *cohabitating*. How much time did either of them have left? Twenty years, maybe, or thirty if they were lucky. This choice carried a weight that the decision to marry Doug at twenty-eight never had, nor had her invitations to various men to join her in bed for a night or a year, nor even switching careers late in life, because a career, after all, was only a career, while a relationship was—

Hilary tipped her head back. The single silver curlicue brushed her neck. She reached up, worked it from her ear, and laid it on the bedside table.

X. Bennington

Why Vermont?

Clem's jaw quivers behind his beard. Hilary thinks he's trying not to cry.

She shrugs. Bennington's a college town. We like college towns. Hilary doesn't need to say Tanya's name; of course Clem knows the other half of the *we* she is referencing.

Just that morning, beginning what she hopes will be the last apartment-packing job she ever does, she found the other curlicue earring at the bottom of a handbag she hardly ever uses. The rediscovery doesn't excite her as much as it once might have.

Later, when Clem leaves for the last time, his absence doesn't upset her as much as it once might have.

This time, she won't entrust the earring box to the moving company. It will ride in the car between her and Tanya. Hilary opens the box now and surveys the jumbled glitter. She'll keep all of these, but she'll certainly buy another pair or two up in Bennington. She doesn't yet own the pair she wants to die in.

■ ■ ■

. . . .

ABOUT THE AUTHOR

Audrey Kalman writes literary fiction with a dark edge, often about what goes awry when human connection is missing from our lives. She is the author of two novels, Dance of Souls and What Remains Unsaid, as well as numerous short stories. She edited two editions of the Fault Zone anthology of California Writers and serves as VP/Speakers for the SF-Peninsula Branch of the California Writers Club. She lives in northern California with her husband, two children, and two cats, and is working on another novel. Visit her website (www.audreykalman.com) and follow her on Twitter (@audreykalman) and Facebook (AudreyKalmanAuthor)

If you enjoyed this book, please share a review and tell a friend!